HER PRISON, HIS GAME

BOOK ONE - A PSYCHOLOGICAL THRILLER AND ROMANCE DUOLOGY

PATRICIA ELLIOTT

ISBN 978-1-7380272-1-7

Published 2024
Published by Patricia Elliott
Her Prison His Game Copyright
2024 Patricia Elliott
Cover design Copyright 2023 Jessica Greeley

Library and Archives Canada Cataloging in Publication

Https://patriciaelliottromance.com

FOREWORD

Please be aware that this book is an intensely dark psychological thriller and contains scenes of violence, abuse, sexual abuse (although done so as delicately as possible), and suicidal moments.

If you are triggered by any of these things, this book may not be for you, and you may wish to move directly on to Book Two, **Beneath His Hands**, which is the romantic suspense portion of this duology. Book Two can be read as a standalone.

This duology was written to show the world how one can rise above any challenges that come their way and can recover no matter how dark the situation is. You can find the strength to rise up and live a life worth living.

CHAPTER ONE

Jenna cringed and dropped her books as a clap of thunder rumbled overhead, shaking the window beside her.

"Miss McCay, if you damage those books, it will come out of your pay cheque," Ms. Hampton said, her dark eyes narrowing. She had her grey hair tied up in a bun and looked a lot like a scary kindergarten teacher with her dark grey three-piece dress suit. The one that made you hide behind your mother on the first day of school.

"Sorry." She knelt down to pick up the books, biting her tongue from saying anything more. The woman acted like she owned the library and wouldn't hesitate to fire her if Jenna responded with a sassy remark. She acted so high and mighty. It wasn't like she hadn't dropped a single book in her life.

Wicked ole' witch!

All Ms. Hampton needed was a broom, and Jenna could envision the old lady flying off into the cloud covered sky. She was probably the one who cast the spell and caused the storm that was pounding the West Coast of British Columbia.

Lightning lit up the room, and she held the books close to her chest, her heart thumping as she waited for the thunder that she knew would come. Damn storm was going to turn her own hair grey before its time. But hopefully she could avoid the grumpy attitude when her time came, unlike the old mistress of the library. Ms. Hampton was probably older than the library itself.

"Teens these days, always careless," the older woman mumbled as she walked away, shaking her head. Jenna stuck her tongue out at her and then quickly closed her mouth when Ms. Hampton turned to face her. "Just for that, you can clean the children's area before you go home tonight."

Definitely a witch!

Children had been coming and going all day. The place was going to be a disaster with garbage everywhere. Because even though parents weren't allowed to bring snacks into the library, they often snuck them in anyway. Why couldn't Ms. Hampton pick on one of the other girls or Derek even? He could do with cleaning the playpen every once in a while. Especially since he needed to be knocked down a peg or two, always thinking he was mister hotshot.

"Seriously, we work in a library and yet somehow he thinks he's god's gift to women," Jenna mumbled.

Ya. Okay. He had the looks, but his attitude stunk. She couldn't wait to get away from them both. The only reason she put up with them was because she needed the money. Her plan was to save up enough money that she could spend a year travelling and seeing the world. She couldn't care less about cute guys or wasting her entire adult life working in some library. Nothing was going to stop her from fulfilling her dream, not even a beady eyed old grouch who watched her like a hawk.

Placing the last of the books on the shelf, she strolled down a side corridor and entered the children's section. The place was virtually deserted and had an eerie Alfred Hitchcock feel to it. She hated this time of day, hated it with a passion. But one more year and she'd be free. Walking over to the toddler play area, she plunked herself down in the soft cushioned chair and laid her head back.

"Just another ye—" Jenna didn't even get a chance to finish her sentence as a loud crack filled the air, shattering the window beside her. She screamed and covered her face. Shards of glass dug into her hands, sharp and painful, as though she'd been stung by a colony of bees.

The wind howled through the window, blowing the papers off a nearby table. Leaves swirled into the room like mini tornados, making an even bigger mess than before. "Great," she groaned. "Just great."

Getting up from the chair, Jenna surveyed the damage. The culprit was a huge branch that broke off a large cedar tree. It was sticking halfway through the broken window. Next to her feet, she saw red marks on the carpet. And when she looked at her hands, she could have sworn she dipped them in tomato soup.

Not good!

So not good. The all too familiar woozy feeling washed over her as her head started to spin. "It's just blood. It's no big deal," she said, taking a deep breath in through her nose and then out through her mouth. "I can do this!"

Would she ever outgrow her fear of blood? Cautiously, she stepped over the glass and moved away from the window. "I'm not a kid anymore. A little bit of blood is no big deal," she mumbled, but her stomach refused to agree as it twisted with nausea. "You aren't dying, you idiot."

"What are you doing bleeding on my floor?"

Jumping at the sound of Ms. Hampton's voice, Jenna turned in her direction, scratching her ankle on the tree branch. Cringing, she came face to face with the woman as a flash of lightning lit up the room. When the adjoining thunder rumbled overhead, she hunched her shoulders. Oh, how she hated storms.

"What happened to my window?" the woman growled. "That one is definitely coming out of your pay cheque."

"It wasn't my fault. The wind broke a tree branch," Jenna said, pointing to the branch on the ground. Its leaves rustling in the wind.

"Don't you dare sass me, girl."

"But, Ms. Hampton, I need the money. You can't charge me for something I—"

"Margaret, darling," Derek said. "How's my angel tonight?"

Jenna shrieked at the sound of his voice, her nails digging into her palm. She hadn't expected anyone else to come barging into the room.

Holy crap.

She really needed a chill pill. Storms always set off her anxiety. All she wanted to do was head home and hide under the covers. The library felt like a crypt with all the spooky shadows lurking around the corners. During the day, it was okay. But in the winter, when it got dark at like four o'clock, it drove her crazy.

Ms. Hampton's eyes brightened, and she beamed a crooked smile in his direction. "Where have you been hiding?"

"Stuck in the archives," he said, winking at Jenna.

The hair on her arms stood on end as a shiver rippled through her. She knew exactly what he meant. It was the resident make out spot, and he had used it to make out with just about every girl in the library. There was a cozy little nook in the back corner that he had claimed as his own.

"Don't worry about the window. I'll get a hold of someone to fix it," Derek said, running a hand through his wayward blond hair, flashing his oh-so-perfect smile.

"Really, dear? You're such a breath of fresh air. You could teach that girl a thing or two," the older woman said, pinching his cheeks before walking away.

"And that, sweet Jenna, is how you deal with Ms. Hampton," he said, sitting down on the arm of a chair.

Jenna rolled her eyes and proceeded to head to the bathroom, which was on the way to the first aid room. She needed to wrap her hand, or she'd bleed all the way there. And there was no way she was going to get down on her hands and knees to scrub blood out of the scuzzy green carpet. The crabby old woman would make her do it too.

The building was silent, but not the usual library silence. It was the creepy one that made you feel like someone was watching you. Maybe it was just the storm, but her nerves were on edge more than normal. It was almost closing time, so the only people left were some die-hard students cramming for an exam, and the employees who were slowly trickling out, one by one.

As she walked into the bathroom, the door swung closed behind her, leaving her in the dark temporarily. "Stupid automatic lights."

Soon, she heard the hum and the room filled with light, making her jump when she saw her reflection in the mirror. Her strawberry blonde hair, more blond than red, was a disaster, bits of glass were stuck in her loose curls. Her clothes were stained with blood. "I'm never wearing a white shirt again."

Turning on the tap, she ran her hands under the lukewarm water and then examined them carefully. It didn't look like any of the cuts needed stitches, thankfully. Not that she could get a good glimpse, though. They kept filling with blood faster than she could rinse them.

Grabbing some paper towel, she wrapped her hands and continued her trek to the first aid room. Another collapse of thunder made her jump. "You're a grown woman, Jenna. Relax."

She was eighteen, almost nineteen. Her birthday was coming up in just a few short weeks. And yet, some people still thought of her as a kid, despite her having graduated high school earlier in the year. They all kept saying she was finally stepping into the real world now. Really? What were the last eighteen years of her life? A virtual reality game?

Shaking her head, she unlocked the door to the first aid room and stepped inside. Well, what else did she expect people to think? She couldn't even get over her fear of thunderstorms and blood. She seemed to be the most nervous person in the world, always waiting for the other shoe to drop.

"Thank you, Mom."

Her mother would wrap her in bubble wrap if she had the means to do so. That was why Jenna had to get away. She needed to get out and see the world, break free from it all. Her mother's anxiety most of all. The last thing she wanted was to be afraid of everything for the rest of her life. And the only way to do that was to take control of her life, live it the way she wanted to.

A sudden sharp jab of pain from one of her deeper cuts made her cringe. Her hands were going to be hard to hide from her mom. If she saw them, she'd freak out and demand that they go to the emergency room to get them checked out. And then, she would never let Jenna go anywhere again. Maybe there were gloves in her locker.

Scrounging through the cupboards, she searched for a bandage. On the top shelf, she found some gauze and non-stick pads and placed them on the counter. Staring at them, she wondered how on earth she was supposed to wrap her own hands. Both were a mess.

Jenna removed the paper towel from her left hand, carefully peeling it away from the spots where it was sticking to her skin. A stinging sensation crawled across every inch of her hand, her eyes watering in response.

Well, there was one upside to all this. She'd get out of doing dishes for a few days. *Oh crap,* she groaned. That would mean telling her mom what happened.

As she started to wrap her hand, the lights flickered. "Please don't go out. Please don't go out."

She kept chanting the words over and over. Praying and hoping the electricity would stay on just long enough for her to finish what she was doing and be on her way home.

Cutting a piece of tape, she slapped it on the side of her wrist, securing the bandage in place. She turned her hand over and examined her poor wrapping job. It wouldn't win any first aid contests, but it should stay on until she got home.

The right hand was going to be a little bit more challenging as she was not left-handed. She was removing the paper towel when she heard a buzzing sound and the lights flickered again. Looking in the mirror on the first aid counter, she noticed that strands of her long hair were pulling away from the rest.

As she was contemplating her whacked out hair style, a loud explosion shook the building, knocking her feet out from under her.

CHAPTER TWO

With the wind knocked out of her sails, she lay there on her back, gasping for air. Stars spun in the darkness above her. Waving a hand in front of her face, a droplet of liquid landed on her nose. She shivered. Either the power was out or she'd knocked her eyeballs out of her sockets. She gently poked one for good measure, and to her relief, it was still exactly where it was supposed to be.

Sitting up, she spotted a sliver of light peeking underneath the door. The generator must have kicked in, turning on the emergency lights. With the stars slowly dissipating, her eyes adjusted to the darkness. Her back ached, and her hands stung like nobody's business.

Thunder rumbled overhead and her chest tightened at the sound. When the rumbling settled, footsteps echoed outside the door. The door handle rattled, making her heart skip a beat. Maybe two.

"Jenna? You in there?"

"Derek?" she asked, her ears ringing. *Anyone but him. Please, anyone but him.* The door swung open and the light behind him cast a shadow that covered her body. He looked twice his normal size. She swallowed hard.

"W-what happened?" she asked.

"Holy shit. You look like hell." He came over and picked her up easily, placing her on the bed. This was a man who could do whatever he wanted to her, and she wouldn't be able to put up a fight. What does he do? Lift weights in his spare time?

He grabbed some paper towel, ran it under the tap, and walked back over to her. He reached up and brushed the damp paper against her cheek. Her muscles tensed.

"Easy, filly."

"I'm not a horse," she said, sitting up a little straighter.

"No, but you're high strung like one."

"Just give me that and get out of here." She tried to snatch the paper towel out of his hand, but he kept it out of her reach.

"Just relax." He ran the paper towel over her face, slowly tracing her lips. "Your face is covered in blood."

She shivered at the contact. She knew what he was trying to do, but it wasn't going to work. He probably thought it was the perfect time for a game of seduction. She may only be eighteen, but *stupid* wasn't her middle name.

Pushing his hand away, she said, "I could use some help wrapping my hand."

Getting knocked up in a library, like a schoolgirl, was not how she wanted to be remembered for the rest of her life. She had plans. Things she wanted to do before settling down, and she had every intention of following through. Letting a guy into her life was not high on her to-do list.

As Derek reached for more bandages, the fire alarm sounded. Jenna jumped. The sprinkler system overhead turned on, soaking them with water. She shrieked while he laughed. Shoving the first aid supplies into his pocket, he took her by the arm and pulled her into the hallway.

"What's going on?"

"I think we were struck by lightning. It must have started a fire," he said.

Sniffing the air, she noticed a faint burning smell. That would explain why her hair had gone whacko prior to the strike. Her mother was going to flip when she got home. That was, if she even got home tonight. She wasn't exactly in the middle of a lucky streak.

As Derek guided her through the library, she spotted something moving in the corner under a bookcase.

"Wait...wait," she said, pulling her arm away from him. "Someone's over there."

"They're just going to have to wait for the fire crews. We have to get out of here." He pointed to the smoke that was seeping underneath the door beside them.

"You do what you want. I'm going to help them." She left him standing there and rushed over, unsure of what she was walking into or what she could do, but she had to try. As she approached the person on the ground, she saw grey hair, trapped in a messy bun.

"Oh my gosh, Ms. Hampton."

The bookcase had landed on her, trapping the lower half of her body underneath. Kneeling down, she touched the older woman on her back. "I'm here to help."

"Get away from me," the woman said in a raspy voice. "Get Derek."

"I'm the one that's here. Not him." Standing up, Jenna pushed on the bookcase. It didn't budge an itch. Giving it another shove, it still didn't move. Moving to the other side, she gripped the edge and pulled. No luck. Leaning over, she rested her hands on her knees, breathing hard.

"Ugh."

Putting her back up against the top end, she placed her hands under the edge and tried to use her knees to lift it. "Where's Superman when you need him?" she grunted.

"Did someone call my name?"

She jumped and fell onto the bookcase, adding more weight to it. The older woman groaned.

"I'm so sorry," Jenna said, apologizing profusely.

"Get her away from me before she kills me."

"Margaret, darling, she is just trying to help."

Finally, between the two of them, they lifted the bookcase off of her. He swept the older lady up in his arms. His actions made Jenna think of a knight in shining armour, and it caused her heart to flutter a little. Not that she would admit that to anyone.

"Let's get out of here," Derek said as he carefully straightened Ms. Hampton's skirt, which had risen dangerously high when he picked her up. Giving them a view neither wanted to see, hairy legs and more.

The smoke thickened, rising into the air above them. She inhaled smoke and doubled over, coughing.

"Come on. We gotta keep moving," he encouraged.

Jenna followed him, and they cautiously moved through the building to the closest exit. Shadows danced along the walls, like fingers waving goodbye as flames spread through the main lobby of the library.

She no longer cared that her blood was still dripping on the carpet. The flames would lick it dry in no time. Holding on to Derek's shirt, Jenna stayed close to him as they stepped around the fallen bookcases. It was almost like they were in the middle of an apocalypse. A shiver ran down her spine, as she half expected a zombie to jump out at her.

Man, she really had to cut down on the horror shows. And it didn't help that her favourite show happened to be The Walking Dead. She couldn't get enough of Daryl Dixon and wished it was his shirt she was holding onto.

They approached the emergency exit and saw wires hanging down in front of it. Hesitant to touch them, she pulled Derek to a stop.

"It's okay, they're dead wires," he said.

"Are you sure?" she asked.

"The power is out, remember?"

Duh!

They were about to go through the exit door when Jenna heard a faint cry for help.

"There's someone else still in here." She let go of his shirt and turned to follow the sound of the person's voice.

"Jenna, leave it. It's too dangerous."

"I can't. Get Ms. Hampton outside." After saying that, she covered her mouth with her sleeve and looked around for the source of the voice. She could hear the sirens as fire trucks approached the building. "Hello, anyone in here?" she called.

"Help me."

At the sound of his voice, a chill passed through her system and goose bumps covered her arms. Wasn't she doing exactly what characters did in a horror movie just before they got their heads chopped off or their stomachs gutted?

"I'm so stupid," she mumbled. Every fibre of her being told her it was a dumb idea, but she couldn't leave whoever it was inside to die. Crouching towards the ground, she tried to escape the smoke that was drying out her mouth and throat, making it hard to breathe. Step by step, she moved towards the sound of the voice.

"Please help me," the deep voice called again.

"I'm coming. Keep talking so I can find you."

If they were trapped under anything heavy, she wouldn't be able to help them. She rounded a corner, coughing as smoke filled her airway. "Where are you?"

"This way, hurry." The voice was stronger this time, and clearly male. It sounded slightly muffled, though. She had to hurry. The smoke was getting thicker by the second. The burning rubber smell was going to taint her taste buds forever.

"Hello?" she called.

"I'm in the Janitor's room," he yelled.

Approaching the door, she tried the handle. "It's locked. Where's the key?" Her heart went into overdrive, her throat closing.

"I don't know."

She still wasn't sure who was locked in the room. He didn't sound like the usual janitor.

"I'll check the lock box," she said. "Be right back."

Rushing to the front desk of the library, she hurried behind the staff counter and checked the lock box. After finding the key, she turned to go back, but tripped over a pile of books. She landed hard, smacking the corner of her forehead on the edge of the counter. The key flew out of her hand, landing who knows where. Dazed, she lay sprawled out on the ground, the room spinning. "Pretty birdies."

Rolling over, she grabbed her head and groaned. If this was her crash course in the reality that would become her adult life, then they could take it back. She didn't want it.

"Fire Department," an unfamiliar voice called out. "Anyone here."

"I am." She gripped the countertop, pulling herself up. A light flashed in her direction, and they rushed over. "There's a man," she said in a hoarse voice, her tongue sticking to the roof of her mouth.

"Where?"

"In the Janitor's room. The door..." She doubled over, coughing, unable to finish her sentence.

"Is there anyone else inside the building besides him?"

"I-I don't kn..." she said, her words partially eaten by another coughing fit.

"Get her outside," one fireman said. "Mason and I will go check the Janitor's room."

Ambulances were already waiting for them when they stepped out the door into the pouring rain. Huge rain drops pelted her forehead, landing on the goose egg already forming between her eyes. One paramedic wrapped a blanket around her shoulders and helped her up into the ambulance, asking the standard twenty questions. All of which she answered without a hitch.

As the guy checked her over and wrapped up her hand, she watched the firefighters bring a bald man outside. Was he the man in the Janitor's room? She didn't recognize him. He wasn't dressed in the usual uniform. He had on a business suit.

But he looked to be in better shape than she was, barely a speck of dust on him. He meandered his way over to her, a smile plastered on his face. When he stopped at the doors of the ambulance, his eyes focused intently on hers, as if analyzing her. She squirmed under his scrutiny.

"I've been told it was you that pointed them my way," he said, pointing to the firefighters. "I just wanted to say thank you."

"You're welcome," she replied.

"What's your name?"

"Jenna."

"I'm Phillip. It's a pleasure to meet you." He stuck his hand out, but then pulled it back when he saw her hands. "I guess you can't shake right now, can you?"

She shook her head.

"You must let me repay you. Can I get your number?"

"There's no need, really," she said, waving off the suggestion with her bandaged hand.

"No, I insist."

She wasn't about to give her phone number to some strange man. "You said thank you. That's enough for me."

"Sorry, sir, we have to go," the paramedic said, climbing into the ambulance. After he shut the doors, they were on their way. The man continued to stare at her through the window, his eyes narrowing.

An uneasy feeling descended upon her, like a dark rain cloud ready to unleash its nasty forces upon the world. Somehow, she didn't think this was going to be the end of her bad luck.

CHAPTER THREE

"I knew I shouldn't have let you take that job," her mother, Iris, said. "I knew something was going to happen."

Jenna rolled her eyes and then winced as sharp pains pulsated behind her left eye, making her groan. All she wanted was to crash into her bed and sleep, but they were sitting in the hospital, waiting for the okay to go home. Pushing a button on the bed controls, she raised the bed to a sitting position, which elicited another groan.

"Are you okay? Do you need more pain meds?" her mother asked, gently touching Jenna's forehead with the ice pack. "Do you know if they gave you a tetanus shot? I better check with the doctor."

Iris was a tiny wisp of a woman, barely five feet tall, but her personality was like a gigantic tornado, whipping everything around in its path. Her short brownish-grey hair was in as much disarray as her anxiety. Jenna found herself exhausted just watching her.

She loved her mom to pieces, but she was ready to live her own life. Be her own person, for once in her life. That's why she took the lousy job to begin with, and why she put up with the gruelling nature of Ms. Hampton.

Her mother put down the ice and walked to the door. "Where is that doctor of yours? I want to speak with him."

"Mom, relax. It's fine, really. I just came to the hospital as a precaution."

"That bump on your forehead says otherwise. You look like you're growing a third eye."

Jenna touched her forehead. She couldn't even imagine what it looked like. It felt like it was about two inches wide and hurt when she raised her eyebrows. She hadn't seen it herself yet and wasn't sure she wanted to.

All she wanted to do was go home and forget all about today. They'd spent the last five hours in the emergency room, which was such a waste of an already lousy day. All because they had the busiest emergency room in British Columbia. And that's even with coming in via an ambulance.

It was one o'clock in the morning now, and the heaviness inside her head was making her feel nauseous and grumpy. She adjusted the bandages on her hand and scratched an irritating itch.

Her mom lightly tapped Jenna's arm. "Don't scratch, it'll become infected,"

Thankfully, the cuts on her hand didn't need any stitches. They just cleaned them and put new bandages on, telling her to monitor them over the next few days. Now, they were waiting on the results from the x-ray of her head, just to make sure she didn't crack her skull or anything. Her vision was a tad blurry, and her hands hurt, but she was pretty good overall.

She'd come so close to getting burned to a crisp, and it unnerved her. People who got struck by lightning rarely lived to talk about it, not to her knowledge anyway. Jenna tilted her head and listened carefully, but she couldn't tell if the storm was still going on or if it had finally moved on.

"Where is your doctor?" Iris asked, pacing the floor of the room.

"Mom, sit down before you wear a hole in the floor. You're making me nauseous."

"I'm going to go get someone."

"Mom, please don't cause any trouble. They'll come in when they can."

This was definitely not one of the most enjoyable nights of her life. She was already tired from everything that happened and trying to keep her mom corralled was getting annoying. If only her dad would have come to the hospital instead, he would have been much more laid back.

But no, he had to be off gallivanting somewhere on the east coast, attending a seminar. He seemed to spend more time away lately, and she had a feeling it was more to get away from her mom than for his job.

The last few months had been rough on the family. Her mom's brother passed away in a car accident, and it completely changed the atmosphere in the house. Her mom didn't want anyone to get behind a wheel, especially Jenna. But when she started her job, a few months back, her dad had bought her a new car. Well, not exactly new. It was a seven-year-old Honda, but her mother was not impressed. She made sure everyone in the house knew about her displeasure.

Jenna, however, loved it. A car meant freedom, and she could use it to do some travelling around the United States and Canada. The only stipulation her father gave her was that she had to pay for the insurance. That wasn't a problem, as she made more than enough to cover the monthly cost. However, with the lightning strike, the library would be closed for months...if not longer. A lump grew in her throat and tears filled her eyes. She was right back where she started.

Her mother's eyes widened, and she rushed over, sitting down on the bed beside her, holding her arms out. "Are you okay? Did you need me to get a nurse?"

Jenna allowed her mom to pull her into a hug. She tried to hold back the tears, her chin wobbling. "S-sorry, I didn't mean to alarm you. It's just the events of the night catching up to me, that's all."

"Oh, baby, I'm so sorry you've had to go through this."

She couldn't hold back anymore and buried her face in her mother's chest, her shoulders shaking with each sob. "It's not fair."

"I know, dear," her mother said, rubbing her back. "I know."

"Well, Jenna," another voice said, breaking into their tender moment. "Your results came back, and it's all clear. You're free to go, but if you find your symptoms getting any worse, please come back and see us."

Not a chance. It would be a cold day in hell before she came back, unless she was dying, of course. And then what did it matter how much time she lost waiting to see a doctor? Time would mean nothing then. But for now, time was everything.

It took almost a week to fully get her vision back, and today was the first day she was headache free. The goose egg was finally disappearing, but her forehead was still black and blue. Even her hazel eyes were looking better, no longer bloodshot from lack of sleep, which surprised her since as nightmares of lightning strikes plagued her for most of the week. She hated storms now more than ever.

Seriously, how many lightning strikes could a person survive in their sleep before it actually killed them? Do people actually die from things like that? She'd heard of people dying from falling off a cliff in a dream, but whenever she had a dream like that, she always hit a trampoline at the bottom before waking up. She shuddered. There was no rest for the weary.

Dabbing a bit of make-up on her forehead, she cringed before continuing to conceal the bruise to the best of her ability. It still hurt like crazy, but, at least, it was looking better.

"Jenna, Cleo is here to see you," her mom yelled, standing at the foot of the stairs.

"Send her up."

When Cleo walked into the room, Jenna was putting on the finishing touches of her make-up. Her best friend was this tall, skinny beauty with long black hair. She had that Egyptian look about her. If she went into acting, it was the part she'd be type-cast for.

"Happy birthday." Cleo gave her a hug and handed her a small box-shaped present. "It isn't much, but I thought it might go with the new black dress you bought."

Opening it, she saw a cubic zirconia in an oval-shaped locket on a sterling silver chain. Inside, she saw a tiny picture of the two of them. It was the one they took on the last day of grade 12.

"I know you have plans on seeing the world. This way I can go with you, too."

"I wish you *would* go with me," Jenna said, her eyes watering.

"No. No crying," Cleo ordered, carefully dabbing at Jenna's eyes with a nearby Kleenex. "You'll smug your make-up, and we've kept the boys waiting long enough already."

"I thought it was just going to be the two of us."

"You only turn 19 once, and I'm taking you to a bar. We need some beefy guys to protect us. Now, come on." Cleo grabbed her arm, pulling her out of the bedroom.

As soon as she stepped out the front door, she knew she'd made a terrible mistake agreeing to go out. Derek stood there, leaning against the car, in all of his playboy glory, sending a god-awful sexy smile her way.

Jenna pulled her arm away and retreated into the house. There was no way she was going to go out now. She would make an utter fool of herself. No guys. That was the deal. Cleo could take it or leave it.

"Nope. No way. Not him."

"Oh, come on, Jenna," her friend pleaded. "It was the only way I could get Jeremy to come. They were hanging out together tonight."

"You know I'm not comfortable around guys."

"Please, for me?"

Unable to refuse the begging puppy dog eyes, Jenna gave in and spent half the evening sitting next to Derek in a dimly lit pub. He kept looking at her oddly, making her incredibly uncomfortable down below. Crossing her legs, she moved a little farther away from him.

"Stop it," she said to him.

"What am I doing?" he asked, wrapping a strand of her hair around his finger.

She smacked his hand away. "You know exactly what you're doing."

Cleo was going to pay dearly for this. Looking out on the dance floor, she tried to spot her dear friend, but it looked like she'd left her high and dry. Derek was the last person on earth she wanted to be stuck with.

"Why don't you go find someone else to torture?" she grumbled.

"But you are so much more fun."

"God, you're impossible." Jenna grabbed her purse and slid out of the booth, desperate to put some distance between them. If she didn't, she'd do something stupid. Spotting the sign for the women's washroom, she made a beeline for the door, her safe haven.

As she put her hands on the door to push it open, she heard someone call her name. Turning around, she saw Phillip making his way over to her. She leaned her forehead against the door and groaned. Why does he keep showing up everywhere? Was he following her?

She shuddered. The intensity in his eyes made her feel uneasy. It felt like he was looking right into her soul. Instead of waiting for him to catch up to her, she fled down the hall and out the fire exit door. She'd celebrate her birthday another day.

Stumbling in her heels slightly and shivering from the cold, she made her way down the dark alley. Wearing high heels and having a few drinks definitely didn't blend together very well. Three Long Island Iced Teas were two drinks too many for her virgin liver.

Slipping on some ice, she landed flat on her butt and groaned. Well, at least that bruise would be in a place no one could see. She stood back up and carefully moved forward, wishing she had grabbed her jacket. But no, she left it inside, next to mister fancy-hands.

Something made a crunching noise behind her, making her jump. Jenna went to spin around, but a strong-smelling cloth was clamped over her mouth and nose. She struggled and struggled, but to no avail. Her vision blurred once again, then her world went dark.

CHAPTER FOUR

W ithout turning the lights on, a dark shadowy figure moved through the lab towards his computer, effectively avoiding all the hard furniture along the way. Sitting down, he begins to type:

First Entry - December 14, 2016
    Phase One
    Subject 013: Jenna McCay
    Age: 19
    Gender: F
    Time: 00:57
    Attending Physician: N/A

    Report:
    Vitals: strong, within normal limits; Physical State: unconscious.
    Subject #013 is currently healthy and has not had an adverse reaction to the chloroform, unlike subject #012. She has been placed in isolation, and the testing will commence as soon as she regains consciousness.
    Subject #013 was in a building that was hit by lightning on

December 7, 2016. She sustained a concussion and had multiple lacerations on her hands. The lacerations on her hands have partially healed. Her forehead is still bruised.

Her mental state, apparent from her evening out with her friends, appears to be normal. She does not appear to be suffering from PTSD (Post-Traumatic Stress Disorder). In phase one, we will observe how she copes with waking up in an unknown location, isolated.

Subject #013 has been injected with a microchip to monitor vitals and movement. Collar B is in place, but not yet active. Interior cameras 1, 2, 3 and 4 are now active.

End of entry.

∼

Jenna opened her eyes and regretted it almost instantly. The bright sunlight made her lean over the side of the bed, puking the remains of her stomach on the floor. She stayed in that position unable to move, her arms hanging down the side, fingers barely touching the floor. The day was not off to a good start at all.

Once her stomach settled, she couldn't help but stare at the wooden floorboards beside her bed. She blinked several times as she ran her hand along the smooth wood, tracing a knot on the board. The last time she checked, she had tan carpet in her bedroom.

What happened last night? Her mind was hazy, and all she could remember was leaving out the back door of the club. Lifting her head, she sat up on the bed. The movement made her head pound and her stomach roll.

She breathed in deeply and then slowly released the air from her lungs. The strong scent of cedar tickled her nose, making her sneeze. Birds chirped outside, welcoming the new day. The only thing she ever heard at home was the annoying woodpecker that had made its home outside her window.

"Cleo?"

Her temples throbbed at the sound of her voice. She squeezed her eyes closed and pressed on the pressure point at the base of her skull to ease the pain. So much for her headaches being a thing of the past. Her hands brushed up against something wrapped around her neck. It was a rubber-like necklace of some sort.

"What the heck?" She never wore neck chokers, not even last night. Opening her eyes, she stood up and swayed sideways. After a minute, she found her balance and glanced around the semi-large room.

The kitchen took up one corner. It had a puke green fridge and matching stove, with a small square table up against the wall that had only one chair. Across from the kitchen was a fraying flower-patterned couch from the eighties that had seen better days. Above the door, leading outside, was an elk-head, antlers and all. And only one word came to her mind. *Rustic*. This had to be a hunting cabin or something.

Somehow, she couldn't see Cleo staying in a place like this. She glanced back around the room and saw the jacket she wore last night sitting on the back of the kitchen chair. There was only one other answer she could think of, and it had to do with the bane of her existence. This was probably his way of getting back at her for rejecting him.

"Derek," she yelled, placing her hands on her hips. "Get your butt out here. Now."

There was no answer. In fact, there were no other sounds in the building but her own. She took a step towards the door closest to her, the floorboards creaking beneath her feet.

She yanked it open and yelled, "Aha."

But the only thing to greet her was a broom covered in cobwebs. Jenna shrieked, jumping backwards as it fell to the floor, her hands flying to her chest. Small spiders emerged from its bristles, crawling back to their hiding spot in the closet.

"Well, if I wasn't awake before," she mumbled, "I certainly am now.

Using the tips of her fingers, she picked up the broom and placed it back in the closet. A strange crawling sensation worked its way up her hand. *Blech. Spiders.* She shivered and wiped her hands on her dress.

"Derek, I'm not kidding around. Get out here."

Again, all she heard were the birds outside. Jenna moved towards the only remaining door along the back wall of the room. It was the only wall with no windows.

She placed her hand on the doorknob and took a deep breath before cautiously opening it. The room was empty, except for an olive-green toilet, a matching sink, and a small bath and shower tucked away in the corner. Where was everyone? Why was she alone?

Pulling at the collar around her throat, she stepped into the small room. She leaned towards the mirror and examined the choker. There didn't appear to be any way of taking it off, and it didn't stretch, so she couldn't pull it over her head.

She never wore stuff like this because it always felt like she was having the life strangled out of her. Maybe that's why someone called it a choker. This wasn't the necklace Cleo bought her, which she knew for certain she had on last night, so where did it come from?

Leaving the bathroom, she went to the window next to the outside door. It had four bars on it, two vertical and two horizontal. Glancing around, she noted that all the windows were the same. Outside, there was a yard, which was surrounded by a thick forest.

She'd never been here before, of that she was certain. How did she wind up here? Where the hell was Derek? Or, for that matter, where the hell was she? With the room beginning to spin, Jenna leaned over and placed her hands on her knees.

Breathe. Just breathe.

There had to be an easy answer for all of this. A logical explanation for why she was here. Did she really drink enough to black out, like the kids at school were always talking about? Reaching for the door handle on the only remaining door she hadn't checked, the outside door, she breathed in through her nose and out through her mouth. It was funny how people could just stop breathing without realizing it, but it was exactly what she'd done temporarily.

She turned the handle and pulled. When the door didn't open, she turned the handle the other way and tried again. The door still wouldn't budge. With her lips pressed together in a firm line, she tried the handle again and this time pushed the door. No luck.

"Damn it, Derek," she yelled, smacking the door a couple times with her palm. "Let me out."

Was this his idea of a joke? Jenna walked over to the window and peered outside. Moving from window to window, she couldn't see anyone moving outside. Her chest tightened, and she rubbed at the ache growing between her breasts.

She pulled her phone out of her jacket pocket and went to dial Cleo's number, but saw the no service signal in the top right-hand corner. She tried to send a text, but it came back with an error message.

Great. Peachy.

Sitting down in the chair, she placed her head in her hands and burst into tears. Her head hurt, her chest hurt, and her stomach made her want to hurl. She'd been so stupid in agreeing to go out with Cleo. Her mother warned her stuff like this could happen. Jenna never wanted to drink again, especially not if Derek was around. He probably thought he could take advantage of her by bringing her out here. Was that why he was never with the same girl twice?

Thankfully, she still had all of her clothes on and didn't feel any different at the moment, so that gave her a bit of hope that nothing happened. But still, here she was...in the middle of nowhere. Alone, with no idea what was going on. Sniffling, she sat up straight and tried to regain control of herself.

Her hand itched, making her glance at it. The area between her thumb and index finger appeared red and swollen, like a bug bite. When she scratched it, something hard shifted beneath her skin.

"What on earth?"

That wasn't there yesterday. A new wave of nausea swept over her body, and she made a mad dash for the bathroom. Man. Could someone send her a new stomach, please? One made of steel would suit her just fine. Her throat burned as she wretched into the toilet, desperately trying to hold her hair back as her body shook under the force of the heaves.

Nope.

No alcohol was ever going to touch her virgin lips again. And when she got back home, she was going to kill Cleo for making her do something she wasn't comfortable with.

The chunky remnants of her last meal swishing around in the toilet bowl reminded her that there was more puke on the floor beside the bed. The very thought of having to clean it up made her stomach roll again.

Forget it.

Derek could clean it up. She wasn't going to touch it with a ten-foot pole. That was the price he'd pay for dragging her out here without her approval. After her stomach finally settled, she rinsed her mouth out with water, then walked into the main room and over to the door again. She turned the handle, hoping for a different outcome.

Still locked.

Examining the window, she pushed it open and poked her head between the bars, trying to see the door. There was a bar across the door with a padlock attached to it. Pulling her head back inside, she narrowed her eyes, her forehead creasing in confusion. None of this made sense.

"Hello, anyone out there?" she yelled, pulling on the bars. There was absolutely no give. They wouldn't budge.

She listened for any signs of life beyond the birds. There were no visible signs of civilization, even the air was untouched. It was as pure as pure could be, and filled with the aroma of the pine and cedar trees that surrounded the property.

She cupped her hands around her mouth and yelled, "Hello?"

The only response was a howl in the distance. The sound wrapped itself around her spine, sending a cold chill through her body. She quickly grabbed the window and pulled it closed, locking the latch. Goosebumps covered her body, and her heart raced.

Jenna stood there, staring outside. There was a nip in the air that reached deep into her bones. She wrapped her arms around her abdomen, unable to stop a shiver from rippling through her. Behind the solid walls, she was safe from whatever animal was lurking outside, but she wasn't sure if that was her greatest threat or if there was an even greater one coming. And she wasn't sure which one to wish for. Hopefully, she'd never have to choose.

But she finally realized one thing.

She'd been kidnapped. And that realization sucked every breath from her body like jumping in a cold, cold ocean in a polar bear swim.

CHAPTER FIVE

Evening fell, and the trees were casting scary shadows along the wall of the cabin. They were like fingers, mocking and laughing at her, telling her no one was coming to save her.

Jenna sat on the bed, leaning against the wall. Her legs were pulled up to her chest as she rested her head against a pillow propped up on her knees, tears flowing unceasingly. They left her. They actually left her behind. Cleo. Derek. Jeremy. Had she meant nothing to any of them? How do you just forget about someone? Why hadn't they come to her rescue? No. It had to be Derek. It had to be. How else would her jacket be here that she'd specifically left at their table?

An owl hooted in the distance. She jumped, banging her head against the wall. "Ouch," she grumbled, rubbing the sore spot. Bats clicked and chirped overhead, making her think of vampires and werewolves. And no sooner had she thought about the creatures of the night, another sound pierced the air, overtaking the rest. A deep and dreadful howl filled the cabin. She wrapped her arms around her legs and held on tight, burying her face in the pillow.

The next howl came from outside the window next to her. Jenna shivered as she knelt on the bed. Grabbing the bars, she looked outside. It was the worst decision ever. Dreadful glowing red eyes locked onto hers. When it tilted its head, a white fang sparkled in the darkness.

She backed away from the window. This had to be a nightmare. A dream. She couldn't really be here. The wolf howled again. Scrambling off the bed, she dropped to her knees in the middle of the cabin and covered her ears, closing her eyes.

"Wake up. Wake up, damn it."

Slowly, she opened one eye and looked around the room. "I don't think we're in Kansas anymore, Toto," she said, tears glistening in her eyes. Whether she liked it or not, this was her reality. She was here as much as she didn't want to be. And that thing was outside. When it howled again, the hair on her arms stood up, erect as a statue.

"You're inside. It's outside," she chanted, trying to reassure herself that she was safe.

Not that her body wanted to listen to reason, though. She had goose bumps on top of goosebumps, and her heart skipped a beat with every horrible howl. There were four walls around her, and a roof over her head. There was no way it could get inside.

It was not like it was a ghost and could walk through walls or anything. It doesn't have the power to transform into anything it wants, right? That only happened in movies, not reality. Not here. Wolves couldn't break into a cabin, not unless they grew hands and could undo a lock. It was just a common, dark grey wolf that had its home in the forest. One that was probably hungry and thought she smelled like a tasty appetizer or a juicy, delectable, out of the ordinary main course.

"Shut up, Jenna," she said, her voice trembling.

Sitting back on her heels, she stared at the dried puke on the floor beside the bed. Surmising that no one else was coming to clean up the mess, she stood up and grabbed the mop out of the closet. She kept her head down low to avoid the eyes that might still be looking in the window and mopped up the chunks of food on the floor.

The howling finally stopped, but that didn't mean he was gone. One thing she learned while babysitting was that if a kid disappeared and was as silent as a mouse, he was likely up to something. It was probably the same with animals of prey, too. He could be stalking her for all she knew.

Rinsing out the bucket, she placed the two items back in the closet. The cabin only had two lights, one was a lamp on the end table beside the couch, and the other was the hanging light in the kitchen. The dim light made the room a little eerie, but she was glad the place had electricity. That meant they couldn't be too far away from civilization, unless it came from a generator somewhere. And she couldn't avoid that possibility, too.

Jenna glanced at the fridge and decided to open it. Slowly. Anything could jump out of its dark confines. When the light came on, revealing a fully stocked fridge of normal everyday items, she sighed in relief. At least one thing seemed normal, but did she dare drink or eat anything here? You weren't supposed to eat food if you didn't know where it came from, but her stomach was rumbling, and her throat was parched.

She reached for a glass and turned it around in her hand, examining every square inch of its surface, not a speck of dirt on it. Biting her bottom lip, she turned on the tap and filled it with water. When the glass was full, she held it up in the air. The water was crystal clear. She held it up to her nose and sniffed it. Nothing appeared to be amiss. Holding it up to her lips, she stuck her tongue in the cool liquid and then ran it along the roof of her mouth. Satisfied, she took a real sip, savouring the feel of the liquid as it slid down her throat.

She went to take another sip but paused in mid-motion when something thumped against the front door, making it rattle. A scratching sound quickly followed. Her hand shook as she placed the glass on the counter. She tiptoed towards the front door and glanced out the window. And there he was, sitting on his back haunches. He turned his long snout in her direction and stared directly at her. She could swear he wanted her to open the door.

"Little pig, little pig, let me in—not by the hair of my chinny chin chin," she said, under her breath.

She pulled at the neck of her dress, hoping it would ease the swollen feeling in her throat that was stealing her oxygen. Being stuck inside the building, with that thing outside, made her feel like the cream inside of an Oreo. She didn't like it one bit. She wasn't a platter to be sampled or a treat to be nibbled on.

Backing away from the window, she searched the cabin for a weapon. The drawers in the kitchen were empty except for a few butter knives, spoons, and forks. No sharp steak knives, nothing.

The scratching continued.

"Go away!" she cried, looking to the left and right for anything she could use as a weapon. The only thing she could find was the handle of the broom. She unscrewed it from the base and held it in front of her.

Finally, the sound stopped. Jenna held her breath, half expecting the creature to come flying in through the window. She checked all the bars, making sure they were secure. When she came to a stop in front of the door again, a cool draft drifted in from underneath and licked the tips of her toes. She shivered. Jack Frost was out in full force tonight.

The person who locked her up obviously knew that. They had put a pile of logs in the corner and set a box of matches on the mantel. She'd never started a fire in a real fireplace before, only flipped a switch at her parents' place to turn on the gas fireplace.

Hopefully, the smell wouldn't let every other creature know there was a meal waiting inside. After putting three logs in the fireplace, she lit a match and tossed it in, watching as it did absolutely nothing. She lit another match and tossed it in. Same thing.

She scratched her head. "Seriously?"

How hard could lighting a fire be? It wasn't rocket science. Her dad had made so many fires when she was little that she should be able to build one with her eyes closed, so why was it being so stubborn now? As she lit another match, an image of her dad kneeling in front of a campfire popped into her mind. The memory brought a tear to her eye. What if she never saw them again? A sob bubbled up inside her, pushing past the lump in her throat.

Crying, she held onto the memory and allowed it to play itself out in her mind. They had gone on a camping trip a few years back, her uncle included. Who knew it would be the last one they would ever go on as a family? Her mother always worried about all the bad things that could happen and refused to just enjoy herself.

In an attempt to make everyone smile, after Jenna's mother's usual complaints, he had tried to make a fire so they could roast marshmallows. That trip was the one and only time the fire was stubborn for him. Usually it started so easily, but his patience was wearing thin with her mom and he couldn't concentrate. Taking the initiative, Jenna had gone out and gathered more small branches for the fire that her father could use as kindling. When she came back with her arms full, he smiled at her. That smile meant the world to her.

Why couldn't things go back to how they used to be? She wanted her normal family back. Heck. She wanted to be in her own bed, not locked in this cabin. Sniffling, she walked over to a bucket in the corner and saw some extra scraps of wood. "Well, that should work."

And sure enough, within five minutes, she had a decent fire going. She pulled the couch over so that it was parallel to the fireplace. Wrapping herself in a blanket, Jenna curled on the couch and revelled in the warmth coming off the glowing embers.

The flames danced like a ballet on Broadway. Mesmerized, she watched them, forgetting all about the trials of the day. What would it be like to be as free as an ember from a fire? Float off into the sunset, away from all the cares of the world. She wanted to fly, to soar, and just be. See everything that the world had to offer before she lost her own mind to anxiety. The fear was there, waiting to take over. She could feel it every moment of every day.

Another thump against the door brought her out of her reverie, her heart racing. "Think rationally."

Last week, she got hit in the head. Maybe she was in a coma, and this was just her fears and anxieties coming to life. Any minute now she'd wake up in a hospital bed, wearing a god-awful gown that could only be tied in the back, flashing her butt to everyone in the world.

That would explain why she hadn't woken up yet. The cabin had to symbolize her trapped mind, and maybe the wolf was her mother trying to hold her back from reaching her true potential. And she had to break out of the cabin to wake up.

Returning her attention to the fire, she blocked out all the sounds from outside. Allowing her body to be lulled by the flicker of the flames, she found her eyes growing heavy. As her eyes closed, and she entered into a much-needed sleep, she didn't see the shadow rising silently behind her.

CHAPTER SIX

"Does she have a boyfriend?" Detective Johnathan Charleston asked as he leaned back in his seat, chewing on the end of his pen. The action drew attention to his brown handlebar mustache, tinged with grey hairs. Not a single hair moved, not even when he opened his mouth to talk.

"My daughter is missing, and you want to know about her social life?" Iris screeched, slamming her hands down on the desk.

"Sweetie, please. Let the man do his job." Daniel McCay took his wife's hand and pulled her back into the chair beside him. Iris had called him earlier, absolutely hysterical, telling him Jenna never made it home last night. That was unusual for his baby girl, even he knew it. She wouldn't stress her mother out needlessly. He tried to call her cellphone, but it went immediately to voicemail.

"Sh-she went out last night with her friends to celebrate h-her birthday," Iris said, wringing her hands on her lap.

The detective raised his eyebrows as he leaned forward, placing his forearms on the desk. "Who was she with?"

"She met up with her friend, Cleo. They were hanging out with Jeremy, and...uh...I think the other boy's name was Derek." Iris pursed her lips together and continued to wring her hands like you would a towel.

"Do you know their last names?"

Daniel and Iris shook their heads. Daniel had seen Cleo numerous times, but he was always too busy doing something and didn't bother to catch her last name. Was this payback for choosing work over his family?

His daughter was turning nineteen, a milestone year, and he was on the other side of the country, attending a conference he really didn't need to go to. He needed air, to be able to breathe for a change. Now, the air surrounding them was more suffocating than ever.

"Do you know where they went?" the detective asked.

"Jolly Jones Pub in Vancouver."

"When were you expecting her back?"

"She was supposed to be back by midnight."

"Could she have gone for a sleepover or maybe ran off with one of the boys?"

Iris put her hands in her hair and pulled, the veins in her neck bulging. "When are you going to stop asking me questions and find my daughter?"

Daniel wished that the hair his wife was pulling out from worrying so much would grow on the top of his own head. He'd started to lose his thick, dirty ash blond hair ages ago. It started with his widow's peak receding and then he was left with the Jean-Luc Picard look.

He placed his hand on top of hers to end her ceaseless wringing. She never used to be this high strung. In her youth, she'd been the life of the party. She was always the first to jump out of a plane or go repelling. Anything that made adrenaline pump through her body. And then everything changed that one fateful day.

"I can't lose her. I can't lose another one." Iris buried her face in his chest.

He kissed the top of her head and wrapped his arms around her. They'd already been through so much. Daniel didn't think his wife could take another hit to her heart. "We know our daughter, Detective Charleston. She wouldn't just run off without telling us. She is a very responsible young woman," he said.

Too responsible sometimes. Teens were supposed to get into mischief. They were supposed to go out and have fun, not be stuck at home and treated like a toddler. That's why he had encouraged Jenna to take the job at the library and even gave her a car. She deserved a life of her own. Even though he wished she could be his baby girl forever, he knew it was time to let her fly.

"We'll send a patrol by Jolly Jones Pub and see if they can find anything on their camera footage. You said she also worked at the library, right?"

They turned and looked at him, nodding their heads.

"Did any of her friends work there?"

"Only Derek, to my knowledge," Iris replied.

"Were they good friends?"

"Not really. They just went out together on her birthday because Cleo begged her," Iris said.

"Okay. I think that is all I need for now. I promise that we'll do everything in our power to find her. With your permission, we would like to search her bedroom and see if we can find anything."

"Sure, no problem." Daniel said, extending his hand to the man.

"Just to clarify, you can be reached at 778-344-6243, right?"

"That's my cell, yes." Daniel answered, then also proceeded to tell the detective his wife's number before putting his arm around her and walking towards the door.

His wife stopped and turned back to look at Detective Charleston. "Please bring my baby home," she cried before running out the door.

Daniel watched his wife flee down the hall. His heart ached for her and for his baby girl. "Thanks for your help." Turning away from the detective, he followed Iris outside. He knew the minute they were behind closed doors, he'd never hear the end of it.

They climbed into the car and Daniel put his key in the ignition. His wife had her face buried in her hands, her shoulders shaking as she cried. He placed his hand on her shoulder, but she shrugged him off, like usual...now that they were away from probing eyes.

Raising her head, she glared at him. "If you would've been here, we could have gone out for dinner like we always do, and she'd still be with us."

With a heavy sigh, he laid his head back on the seat. Things were difficult already, and he didn't need to be in a battle with her, too. He didn't have the heart to fight anymore. Everything always seemed to be his fault.

"I'm sorry," was all he said. What else could he say? She was right. That was their birthday tradition. A tradition they had honored ever since their daughter was old enough to sit in a restaurant, besides taking her swimming or to an indoor playground. "I'm going to drop you off at home and go look around."

"Can we stop by the graveyard first?"

"Sure, whatever you want."

Detective Johnathan ran his hands down his face. That was the thirteenth disappearance in the last six months, and each victim was from Surrey. He pulled on the curl of his mustache, staring at all the faces looking up at him from his desk. They all disappeared without a trace. There were no phone calls. No ransom notes. And no witnesses.

He wasn't sure how he knew it, but his gut told him all the vanishings were connected. And the person responsible seemed to favor women. Only four out of the thirteen victims were male and all the victims were between thirty to fifty years old, except for Jenna. She was the first person under twenty. That meant age wasn't the deciding factor, so if he wasn't barking up the wrong tree, what made the kidnapper go after her?

The job titles of the victims didn't even give him anything to go on, either. They were as broad as broad could be. One was unemployed, another was a doctor. There were no common themes. Only a common location—Surrey.

The part that upset him the most was that he didn't even know when the next disappearance would happen. The guy didn't run on a schedule, like so many serial killers. Sometimes he waited two months. Sometimes only a month. This time, it had only been a week since the last abduction. What next? Tomorrow? Was it based on how long his victims lived for or was there another clock he followed?

Picking up Jenna's picture from off his desk, he studied her. She was wearing her cap and gown, fresh out of high school, ready to live her life. There was nothing special about her appearance specifically. She wasn't drop dead gorgeous, but she had that homely look about her, gentle and kind to a fault. Innocent. He glanced back at the other faces of those who were missing.

It irked him that none of the bodies or persons had ever turned up. They were all missing in action. So, either they were alive or there was a mass grave somewhere. As much as he wished he was wrong, he was guessing it would be the latter.

It is hard to believe in this day and age of technology that people could disappear without a trace. Everyone had cell phones that could be tracked via the Global Positioning System, and yet, his techs couldn't get a lock on them.

They had all this equipment, but what good was it if they couldn't find anyone? Growling, he threw his pen across the room. It was his job to find people, but right now the bad guy was winning, and he felt like he sucked at his job. He had a fairly good batting average over the years, but this year he was hitting zero for thirteen.

John didn't like losing. And he was determined not to lose this time. He'd find whoever was responsible and put them away for a long, long time. They wouldn't even remember their own name when he was done with them.

A brown-haired head peeked around the corner of the door frame. It was his partner, Clyde Rivers. "A few of us are going out for a drink. You in?"

"If you want to go for a drink, can you guys go to Jolly Jones Pub? I want you to see if you can get ahold of their camera footage. I'm going to take Wynn down to Daniel McCay's house and see if we can find any leads."

"You are probably going to need a court order for them to release the footage."

"Just see what you can do. It's already been 24 hours since her disappearance. We don't have a moment to lose. If they give you any trouble, we'll go down to the courthouse tomorrow."

"Are you sure you don't want to come?"

"Not tonight, but thanks. I'm going to get the search done at their place and then get home to my family." He needed to hold his daughter until she fell asleep, and then hold his wife in his arms and make love to her until he couldn't feel his limbs anymore.

Life was too unpredictable. Things could change at any moment. One day, everything could be fine, and the next, your world could be turned upside down. He faced that reality in his line of work every day.

He was going to find Jenna and bring her home. He wasn't going to stop until he'd turned over every rock and searched in every crevice. John would treat Jenna as if she were his own daughter.

The McCay family had already been through enough. They deserved one good outcome in their lives. And he was going to make sure they had it. Christmas was coming, and he could think of no greater present than for a family to be reunited.

Grabbing his jacket and Stetson hat off the hook, he strolled out the door with purpose and determination. It was time to catch the jerk behind the disappearances once and for all and bring him to justice.

It was Detective Charleston's turn to rise. He wasn't going to stop until the man was caught. One way or another, the perpetrator was going down.

That was a promise.

Jenna blinked rapidly as she stared at the spot beside her on the couch, her heart leaping into her throat. Sitting there on the cushion was the necklace Cleo had given her. She reached out to grab it, but then pulled her hand back, as if it were a rattler poised to bite. It wasn't there before. She was sure of it. When she turned her head, a slight musky odour caught her attention. She gasped.

Someone was here.

Frozen in her spot, she craned her head and listened carefully. But the only sounds she could identify were the rumblings of the noisy fridge and the pounding of her heart. Not even the fire crackled anymore. Only a few glowing embers remained. Turning, she knelt on the couch and looked around the cabin.

She tried to take a deep breath, but it stopped in her throat. It was like a boa constrictor had wrapped itself around her lungs. With short, uneven breaths, she stood up and tip-toed to the bathroom door, which was slightly ajar.

The floor creaked beneath her feet. Jumping, she spun around and then let out a long breath when she didn't see anyone there. Continuing to the bathroom, she stood outside and listened. There didn't seem to be any sound coming from the small room. She pushed the door open.

Empty

Backing away from the bathroom, she couldn't shake the unease that someone had been in the room with her. They may not be there now, but it still felt like eyes were burrowing into the back of her head.

She walked over to the front door and tried the handle. No luck. It was still locked. Hitting the door with her palm, she cried, "Let me out."

Stupid. Dumb. Idiotic.

Why on earth had she agreed to go out with Cleo? She knew better than to go to a pub in downtown Vancouver. Backing up a little, she kicked the door, which caused her ankle to pop, sending a sharp pain up her leg. Unfortunately, the door didn't budge.

"That smarts," she mumbled, rubbing her ankle.

She tried again. This time with her shoulder, but she ended up bouncing right off the wood, landing on her butt. Tears filled her eyes as she sat there on the cool floor, her shoulder and ankle throbbing.

"I wanna go home," she cried into the empty air around her. "Do you hear me? I want to go home."

"No," a computerized voice said, echoing throughout the room.

Her whole body tensed, and her jaw dropped in surprise. Someone was listening to her. She hadn't expected a reply and was at a loss for words. Was it the same person who came into the cabin while she was sleeping?

"W-who are you?" she asked.

No reply.

"Why did you bring me here?"

Silence filled the room.

"Please tell me where I am. Why did you bring me here?" No matter what she asked, the voice wouldn't speak again.

Standing up, she said, "Damn it! Answer me!" If someone was talking to her, there had to be a speaker somewhere. And if they were listening to her, could they be watching her?

She wrapped her arms around herself self-consciously. She had no desire to be on stage, or to be the centre of attention, but that's exactly what it felt like. "Derek, if that's you, please let me go. I'm sorry I blew you off."

Again, no reply.

"Okay, fine. Ignore me."

Was this his way of getting back at her for not showing any interest? With what she knew about him, he'd be just the type of guy to pull this sort of prank. Get her scared, worried, and then come riding in like some handsome hero in her dreams.

There was no way she was going to give him the satisfaction. If it really was him watching her, and she had a sneaky suspicion it was, she was going to keep her cool. Let him think she was fine. He had left her in a nice warm cabin, stocked with food. There could be worse fates, right? He could have locked her in a damp, cool dungeon, handcuffed to the wall, but he hadn't.

She just wished he would have thought of a television or something. There was absolutely nothing to do here but sit and think. There were no paperback books, nothing physically available to keep her entertained. Thankfully, she had a few ebooks on her phone, but those wouldn't last her long and neither would her phone battery. Given that she didn't know how long she'd be here for, she'd have to spread things out a little.

Jenna walked over to the window and looked outside. Fresh snow had fallen and covered the ground, sparkling in the sunshine. Despite the circumstances, it did look pretty. Glancing towards the door, she noticed there were no footprints in the snow leading to the cabin. No evidence of anyone approaching the cabin unnerved her. Had it snowed more while she was asleep after they had gotten into the cabin?

Why hadn't she woken up when they came inside? Wouldn't she have heard the lock and the door being opened? Unless this was all a coma dream like she thought, and sounds worked differently here. She pinched her arm and then twisted the skin. Yelping in pain, she rubbed the burning sore spot and shivered as a chill ripped through the air. Jenna glanced at the fireplace. With the fire having burned itself out, the cabin would become its own winter wonderland before long. Grabbing a few more logs, she started another fire. Another few days of this, and she'd be a fire-making pro in no time.

Standing up, she wiped her hands on her dress just as her stomach rumbled, reminding her she hadn't eaten anything in over twenty-four hours. Rummaging through the cupboards, she spotted some unopened cereal and in the back left corner a can of hot chocolate.

After preparing her food, she curled in front of the fire, this time with a bowl of cereal and a cup of hot cocoa. Munching on the food, she wondered what her mom was thinking right now. What did Cleo and Derek tell her when they came back without her? Did they even let her family know, or was Cleo too trapped in her own desires to even notice she was gone? Or Cleo probably thought she just went home without her.

Did her dad know? Had he flown back to Surrey when he found out his only daughter was missing? Jenna sniffled. She had to find a way to get back to them. If Derek didn't come back soon and show himself, then she would find a way out of this cabin herself. Someway. Somehow. She had no intention of spending her Christmas in the middle of nowhere.

And the next time she saw him, she would knock his ass into kingdom come. For now, it was a matter of killing time and thinking of ways she'd make him pay for dragging her out here.

It had to be him because thinking that way was the only thing keeping her sane. And he wouldn't hurt her. Would he?

Ha

He left a pile of broken hearts in the wings of the library.

The next morning, something crinkled beneath her feet as she did a full body stretch over the length of the couch. Sliding her legs off the cushions, she sat up and glanced down beside her.

Staring up at her was a big bold picture of herself on the front page of 'The Province,' her graduation picture, no less. Her heart rate increased, and her fingers gripped the edge of the cushion, knuckles turning white.

He was here.

Again.

The headline read, 'Missing Surrey Teen.' As she read through the article, a lump grew in her throat and tears burned her eyes. Her mom was begging for her return. They even mentioned Derek, Cleo, and Jeremy as being the last people who saw her before she disappeared. She couldn't help but focus on the words of her mom.

"She's my only baby left. We already lost one. I can't lose her, too. Please let her go."

The words bounced around in her head like a ping-pong ball. What did her mom mean? She was an only child. There were no others. None that she knew of, anyway. They didn't even have any other pictures around the house. Wouldn't they have told her if she had a sibling? How could they have kept her in the dark if that was true? And if Derek brought her out here, why wouldn't he have told her parents? Were his plans more nefarious than she first expected? Or...

What if it wasn't Derek?

No. No. It had to be. It couldn't be anyone else. She didn't want to think about it being anyone else. They were all together at the pub, and he was doing this to get back at her.

What if it's not him?

Damn it. She hated sentences that started with *'what if.'* They should be banned from existence. Anxiety always rode in on those types of questions. The scary part was that she had to face the question because there was a possibility it wasn't him. And if it wasn't, then who was it? Was it someone else she knew? What if it was Phillip?

And how the heck did they keep getting into the cabin without her hearing them? They've been able to sneak in twice now without waking her up. And like yesterday, there were no footprints in the snow. No indicator that anyone had walked in from outside with wet boots.

Just what the heck were they, a ghost or something? A witch who could fly? Maybe that explained the broom in the closet. Jenna paced the cabin, unnerved. It was Day three, and she still had no idea why she was here.

The paper said she was the thirteenth Surrey resident to disappear, and the reporter had asked the police whether the same perpetrator was involved in them all. And the police just said they were looking into all possibilities and angles. But, apparently, the police already had a suspect, and they were hoping to wrap her case up quickly. She wasn't sure how much of that was bullcrap, but she'd hold on to that hope with a vice grip.

She had a sneaky suspicion that Derek was their number one suspect currently, but with each passing moment she grew more unsure as to whether he was behind her disappearance. He was a dickhead, sure, but she highly doubted he'd make her parents worry like this. With everything they'd been through, it just didn't fit his personality. He was a people person, liked wrapping everyone around his finger.

Backing up towards the bed, she sat down on the edge and lifted her head to the ceiling. "Please, don't let it be a stranger."

She'd never been much of a believer in her life, but she could certainly do with God's help right about now. When she was little, she went to church with her grandmother, not so much now though. If God could get her out of this, she'd worship him for life.

As she stared at the ceiling, she noticed it was a triangle-shaped design, leaving no room for an attic. That meant there was no sneaking out through the roof. Was it the same in the bathroom? Walking into the small room, she saw the ceiling was lower, almost like the bathroom was an after-thought in the design.

On the ceiling was a square fan, surrounded by what looked like particle board panels. Standing on the toilet lid, she pushed a panel out of the way and stuck her head into the attic. She could barely see over the panel. Placing a foot on the counter, and another on the back of the tank, she hoisted herself up higher.

Nothing much was up there, except the rest of the fan, pipes and some wiring. The roof was the same triangle one as in the rest of the cabin, except she could get a little closer to it from inside the bathroom. Pulling herself up, she tested the strength of the wooden beams before sitting on one.

If she'd known she was going to become an acrobat, she would have worked out more. *Phew.* Jenna wiped her brow before proceeding to balance precariously between the two beams as she reached for the ceiling, which was only a foot above her head. It was, unfortunately, as solid as a rock.

Defeated, she dropped down, plunked herself down on the toilet seat, and kicked the door of the cabinet, chipping off some of the tacky green paint.

"I just can't catch a break," she growled.

Walking towards the couch, she looked down at the picture of herself. Two nights in a row, the creep had entered the cabin. Both nights she was sleeping. Not tonight though. She had no intention of falling asleep. She would stay awake and when he came into the cabin, she'd be waiting for him.

He wasn't going to know what hit him.

CHAPTER EIGHT

I n his own mind, he referred to himself as the 'The Scientist,' although others would call him anything but. He had his own way of doing things, hands on so to speak. Here, there was no one to tell him what he could and couldn't do, or tell him how far he was allowed to go. He was his own boss.

No limits, and that was what he liked. It allowed him more freedom to gather his information, and Jenna was proving to be a delightful surprise. He knew she would make a good test subject. Most thought the worst immediately, but despite her anxiety, she was handling things rather well so far.

But he was about to switch things up a little and couldn't wait to see how she handled the second round of testing. It was a good thing he'd activated the collar last night. He wouldn't have had a chance tonight. She was refusing to fall asleep.

It was zero-two hundred hours, and she was pacing the cabin. Her vitals were still good, despite occasionally spiking. She was probably waiting for him to show up again, but that wasn't going to happen this time. He had something else in mind. Now, it was a matter of figuring out how to do it while his little jewel was awake.

Maybe he should wait until she exhausted herself and couldn't stay awake any longer. He had time to kill and wasn't in any great rush. It's not like anyone could track him, anyway.

He had been a little worried about taking another person so soon, but his work couldn't wait. In truth, he couldn't wait. Not having someone at his disposal always drove him crazy. This was like his own personal video game, live reality.

She had a real beating heart and an incredibly nice body, which he couldn't wait to get to know more intimately. A little drool gathered at the corner of his mouth as he rubbed his hands together with anticipation.

He finished entering his updated information into the computer and then hit save. There really had been nothing new to report, except for her little escapade into the bathroom's attic. None of his other test subjects thought of doing that. It was a good thing he fixed the roof before bringing her in. One board had been extremely loose for years.

"Go to sleep, my newest angel."

His own eyes were growing heavy, but he needed to finish setting things up before getting some much needed shut-eye. And that required his test subject to go to sleep, but short of forcing her, there wasn't much he could do.

He wasn't ready to reveal himself yet. He wanted her to draw her own conclusion as to what was going on because the element of surprise was the name of his game. Watching them figure things out was such a rush. Getting right in there and pushing them to their limits felt much like sky-diving for him. It made him feel alive, unlike the other corpses rotting in the walk-in freezer.

He would have to get rid of them eventually, bury them after the snow melts. The Winter season had been strangely brutal this year, and it was causing more trouble than usual for him. Between the thunder and snow storms, it was hard to do everything he wanted to do. The southwest coast was known for its milder weather, which was why he had moved down here in the first place. After he was done with Jenna, it would probably be a good idea to wait a while for the weather to clear up before trying again.

Returning his attention to the monitor, he noticed she had taken up residence on the couch again, in front of a newly made fire. Soon he'd have to find a way to restock the firewood. He didn't want her to freeze before he'd completed his research. He watched as she leaned forward and ran a hand through her hair.

She had the silkiest hair of any woman he'd ever met. He couldn't stop running his hands through it when he had placed her on the bed a few days earlier. Even her skin was soft to the touch, and his crotch stirred to life as he thought about touching her again soon. She was his for the taking.

No one had ever turned him on so much. Who knows, maybe she would even come to love him. He'd read about Stockholm syndrome and wondered if there was any truth to it. None of the older women had developed it, which was one reason why he decided to try young, naïve, and innocent Jenna.

He licked his lips. This research project was definitely going to be the most fun he'd had with anyone. She had finally stopped moving around, but her vitals still showed her to be awake, but maybe if he was super quiet, she wouldn't even know he was there.

Time for phase two...

Jenna glanced down at the time on her cellphone, it read six in the morning. The muscles along the sides of her neck had started to tense up over the last hour, and a headache was brewing behind her eyes.

Wasn't he coming?

No matter how long she stayed still on the couch, without moving a muscle, he didn't show himself. It was eerily quiet. Even the wolf that had visited her previously hadn't made an appearance. He was usually pretty vocal with his howls, but not tonight.

She wasn't sure how much longer she could stay awake. Every pore in her body cried out for sleep. Her biological clock didn't allow for all-nighters. Usually when the clock struck ten at night, her body went into hibernation mode. She couldn't even stay awake long enough to look at her phone for ten minutes. It usually dropped out of her hand and hit her in the face.

Of course, that meant she was an early bird, which really was the best time of the day in her opinion. She loved watching the sunrise with all the various colours swirling around the sky as the sun rose to greet the day. It was the only peaceful time in her parents' house, although being in the city, it was never super quiet.

In a way, she yearned for the noises of the city right now. The utter silence surrounding her had a spooky and eerie feel to it. There was no doubt it could have been serene and breathtaking if the circumstances were different, but they weren't.

Metal clinking behind Jenna caught her attention.

"That's new."

She narrowed her eyes and glanced around the cabin before turning her attention to the front door. The only time she heard something that close was when the wolf came for a visit. A sudden soft thud against the door made her jump.

With her heart pounding, she backed as far away from it as possible until her back hit the kitchen counter. Someone or something was out there. And she had a sneaky suspicion it wasn't the wolf. He was always gone by this time.

Then, as quickly as it all started, the sounds stopped. Biting her lip, she tip-toed towards the front door. She stopped with every step, listening to the sounds around her. As she neared the window, she drew in a shaky breath.

Squinting her eyes, she tried to see outside, but it was still dark. *Oh, the joys of winter.* The light inside the cabin didn't reach very far beyond the glass, and she couldn't really tell what was going on outside. There was no movement that she could see.

She wasn't taking any chances though. Jenna walked to the other side of the couch and pushed it towards the front door, blocking it from opening. Why hadn't she thought of doing that last night?

Turning around, she plunked herself down on the cushion and took a few slow, deep breaths, trying to calm her heart. If she couldn't get her anxiety under control, she'd have a gosh darn heart attack before she turned thirty. And she had every intention of living until she was a hundred years old.

To take her mind off the new noises, she opened the Kindle app on her phone and scrolled through her selections. There were a range of books from romance stories to horror novels. Given her current situation, she opted out of the horror novels and picked a romance book instead. She'd probably read every single romance story that was in their library back home and had been trying to push for some newer material, but no luck so far. Thank goodness for Kindle.

Hours later, her eyes shot open, and she found herself sprawled on the couch, hands on her chest with the phone cradled between her breasts. Springing up to a sitting position, she gasped and slapped the cushion. She had tried so hard not to fall asleep. Damn her internal clock. Jenna quickly glanced around the room. There didn't appear to be anything different this time. Nothing amiss. Sunbeams shone in through the windows, creating a pathway on the floor.

Kneeling on the arm of the couch, she looked out the window and glanced around the yard. The snow was sparkling like diamonds in the sunlight, but it was strangely untouched.

"Weird."

In the far corner of the yard, she saw movement in the trees. She wiped away the fog on the window, attempting to get a better look. But it was nothing more than a deer out for its morning jaunt. Overhead, birds were flying, probably out looking for their morning meal. Everything else seemed normal. Even the wolf's paw prints from the other day were all gone, covered by the freshly fallen snow. There were no new tracks from whatever visited her earlier.

She leaned forward, pressing her face against the bars, and glanced towards the front entrance of the cabin, her eyes widening. The padlock and bar were both gone. Jenna got up and pushed the couch back to its normal spot. Her luck was looking up today. Maybe Derek had finally decided to let her go.

Gingerly, she reached for the handle and turned it. The cabin was an okay vacation place, but she wouldn't want to live here permanently. It would get old super fast. She pulled on the handle and to her surprise the door opened.

Standing off to the side, she poked her head out the door, scanning her surroundings. She felt totally and completely exposed for the first time since she woke up here. How was she supposed to know where to go, especially when she had no idea where she was? What if her captor re-locked the cabin, and she couldn't get back inside if she needed to?

No. She wouldn't ever go back inside, being outside gave her a fighting chance to find her way back to civilization. All she needed to do was find a spot with cell service so she could call someone to come and get her. Chewing on her lip, she pondered which way to go. What if she couldn't find anything and needed to come back? How would she find her way back?

Crumbs.

People in movies always left a trail so they could find their way back and not get lost. Jenna walked over to the cupboard and grabbed the oatmeal crisp cereal. Animals might eat the cereal, but it should hopefully do the trick.

Putting on her jacket and carrying the box of cereal, Jenna took her first tentative step outside the shoebox cabin. Deciding to take a direct path, she went straight ahead as fast as her feet could carry her in the knee-deep snow.

As soon as she reached the property line, a strong electric shock threw her backwards, knocking her flat on her back as sharp wavelike pains coursed through her neck. She pulled at the collar, gasping for air.

Her lungs burned for oxygen, her vision blurring. "Someone help me," she mouthed silently, unable to cry out as her throat kept constricting with each new jab of pain. Jenna clawed at the collar, tears trickling down her cheeks.

With all oxygen and energy spent, her eyes rolled into the back of her head and everything went dark.

CHAPTER NINE

Jenna ran her hand down her chest and in between her thighs, pulling her hand away quickly. She was *naked*, except for a comforter draped over her. She turned her head to look around the room, but a burning pain stopped her in mid-turn. With a shaky hand, she gingerly touched her neck and winced. Her skin beneath the choker felt rough to the touch, as though her skin was peeling.

As she leaned on her elbows to push herself up, a ribbon of pressure tightened around her head, and Jenna groaned. Every muscle in her body protested the movement. Beneath her chest, her heart raced, apparently wanting to squawk as much as the rest of her. Breathing heavily, she forced herself to sit up.

"I'm too young to feel like this."

That's when she smelled it.

Him.

He was here again. She pulled the flat sheet off the bed and wrapped it around herself, her breath hitching. Why did he take her clothes off? Did he...

Oh God

A wave of dizziness washed over her, adding to the nausea

building in her belly. She jumped up to rush to the bathroom but fell to her knees. Her legs were too weak to support her weight.

Jenna didn't feel any different down there, but her whole body was on fire. So would she even know if they had violated her? Lying there on the floor, she curled into a ball. She'd been outside, running towards the forest. Now she was back inside. Stiff, sore, and naked.

"Mommy," she whispered, her lower lip trembling. If he touched her...

Oh god!

She couldn't even contemplate the idea. Reaching down, she touched herself, then looked at her fingers.

No blood.

She sighed in relief, but her heart join in. It kept thumping as if it was in the race of its life. If he violated her, there would be blood. That must mean her hymen thingy was still intact.

"I hope."

But what did she know? She was a virgin, completely untouched by any man. The thought of rape kept bouncing around in her head, unable to fully shut it off. Images of a naked man grinning wickedly took over her mind. He was reaching for her, drool dripping down his chin.

She plugged her ears and squeezed her eyes closed. "Stop it. Stop it!"

Her blood pounded in her ears, and her heart continued to beat wildly, her breathing short and shallow. It was like something out of her worst nightmare. Every movie that had a cabin in the woods flooded her mind. Their stories were coming to life before her eyes.

And they never ended well. Everyone usually died, or just about everyone. Whoever was left often found themselves in an insane asylum. *Oh god.* Why did she have to be an expert on horror movies? She hit the side of her head with her palm, trying to knock out the bad thoughts.

Shivering from the cool air coming between the floorboards, Jenna sat up and groaned. Did anyone catch the number of the truck that hit her? Her muscles twitched as she stood up. She pulled the sheet flush against her body and glanced around the room. Her clothes were nowhere to be found.

Her jacket, however, was resting on the chair as if she had never moved it, and her shoes were underneath. There were new logs next to the fireplace and a small fire burning in the fireplace, which was dying. He must have started it for her.

Jenna wandered over to the door and tested the handle. Sure enough, the door opened like before. She shuddered as a breeze made the sheet flutter around her, exposing her legs to the chilly winter air.

She pushed the door closed and walked over to the kitchen. Thankfully, her crotch wasn't aching. That knowledge relieved her fear slightly, as it likely meant no one took advantage of her.

But that didn't mean it wouldn't happen. She had to run. It was going to be cold without her clothes, but she had no plans on waiting around until he used her body for some other cringe worthy activities.

Putting on her shoes, she grabbed her jacket and wrapped the sheet around her legs and rushed out the door, deciding to go to the left this time. Her muscles ached with each step, but she kept moving, growing leery as she neared the tree line.

When she was about ten feet away, the collar around her neck buzzed, vibrating slightly. Jenna swallowed hard, her hands growing clammy. She continued to press forward, albeit a little more slowly this time.

Five feet away, a small jolt of electricity emanated from the collar, zapping her already tender skin. "Okay. Fine!"

Turning around, she tried the opposite direction, to no avail. She only had one direction left. Her legs were freezing and the draft reaching her crotch didn't feel too pleasant. She wouldn't be surprised if she wound up with icicles in places she'd rather not mention.

Jenna stopped ten feet away from the forest, waiting for another jolt, but it never came. One slow step at a time, she allowed herself to move closer to the pine trees in front of her, her heart racing.

Still nothing.

Stopping, she listened for any sounds of life, from people to vehicles, but all she could hear were birds singing and the sound of water running. The forest was much denser in this direction. It wouldn't be an easy trek and her legs were going to hate her for this. Entering the wooded area, she pushed her way through the low-lying bushes, ignoring the thorns clawing at her legs. The taste of freedom rested on the tip of her tongue. She couldn't believe it. She was free at last.

Excitement rushed through her, making her move even faster, until the ground beneath her feet disappeared, and she found herself falling.

"I didn't do it." Derek said, pacing the small interrogation room like a caged cat.

"You were the last one to see her on the night she disappeared," Detective Charleston said, lifting the two front legs of his chair off the floor as he leaned back, watching the youngster's reaction, his feet crossed on his desk.

"We went to the bar to celebrate her birthday. She ran off."

"Why would she run off?"

"Hell if I know," he said, running a hand through his hair, looking perplexed.

"Did you try anything?"

Derek stopped pacing and looked at him. "Like trying to pick her up, you mean?"

Johnathan tilted his head and asked, "Did you?"

"Well, ya, but what does that have to do with anything?"

"Walk me through what happened that night." John bet his bottom dollar she rejected him. The boy may be what girls defined as 'hot,' but from what he had learned about Jenna, she was too smart to fall for a surfer boy. Derek was the type of kid that probably had a different girl every week.

Derek walked over to where Johnathan was sitting and placed both palms flat on the table, looking directly at him. "I already told you what happened. We went to the bar. Jeremy and Cleo disappeared, god knows where, leaving me with Jenna. She didn't care for my advances and ran away from our table. I went looking for her, but couldn't find her. Happy?"

The boy stood up and shoved his hands in his pockets, hanging his head. "Sorry. I'm just worried about her."

It didn't look like Derek was lying, but Johnathan wasn't ready to cross him off the suspect list yet. Everyone would remain a suspect until the girl was safely back home.

"Do you know of anyone who was angry or upset with her, besides yourself?"

"The only person I know who doesn't like her is Ms. Hampton."

"Did you notice anyone stranger hanging around the library while she was working?"

"Well, there was a man that made her uncomfortable on the day of the storm. I think she called him Phillip. She found him trapped in the Janitor's room and said he kept asking for her number."

"Did she give it to him?"

"No. He even came up to me after the ambulance left and asked if I knew how to get in touch with her."

"If I got my sketch artist in here, do you think you could describe him?"

Derek nodded his head and let out a long breath, his muscles visibly relaxing as he plopped his butt down on the seat across from John. "Detective, while I may not be her favourite person, I would never hurt her. I like her."

"But her rejection hurt you." The pain in the kid's eyes was plain to see. He masked it quickly, but it was there. "Why pursue someone who isn't interested in you?"

"She's interested, but scared."

John stroked his chin between his thumb and index finger. That was an interesting revelation. "How do you know she's interested in you?"

"A man knows."

"Kid, if a woman was that easy to read, no guy would ever be kicked in the balls."

Men have been clueless about the women folk ever since the dawn of time. And just when they thought they were about to figure them out, the ladies confused them all over again in some way, shape, or form. They were an enigma designed to keep men on their toes.

His wife surprised him regularly and helped him stay grounded, even if that meant knocking him up the side of the head. God knew he needed a swift kick in the ass every once in a while. That's what this boy needed, a woman to kick him in the ass and bring him down off his arrogant high horse. But was he arrogant and conceited enough to do something about being rejected? Could he have kidnapped Jenna?

"Does your family own any other property?"

"My parents lived in Ontario, where they own a house. Me, I'm just renting a small flat in North Surrey."

"What made you move across Canada?"

"To live my own life, I suppose."

He could remember those years, wanting to get out from under your parent's wings. Some parents were far too overbearing. The shorter the leash, the greater the desire was to get as far away from them as possible.

"You couldn't do that there?" John asked.

Derek tapped his fingers on the table impatiently. "No, not really."

Taking a sip of his coffee, John studied him, waiting for him to continue. When it was clear the boy wasn't going to say anything else, he asked, "Estranged?"

Derek shrugged his shoulders and pressed his lips together firmly. Detective Charleston knew there was a story there but decided not to pursue it at this point. He'd already kept the boy at the office for a few hours, watching his reactions.

"We can talk more about that later. Let me go grab the sketch artist. Once you guys are done, you're free to go. Just don't skip town."

In no time at all, Christopher, the department's resident sketch artist, dropped the picture on his desk. The face staring up at him took him by surprise. It was the last person he expected to see.

His ex-partner.

CHAPTER TEN

Dazed and confused, she lay there in a heap. It was official. Everything was out to get her. There was no doubt in her mind. Her eyesight took a few minutes to come back into proper alignment. When it finally did, she took in her surroundings.

She'd fallen into a pit, much like the type you'd use to catch an animal. The hole had been covered by thin branches that broke when she had stepped on them. The ground beneath her was uneven and soft, and a rotten odor steam-rolled its way into her nostrils.

Reaching down, her hand came in contact with soft, velvety fur. Her eyes widened, and she gasped. She didn't want to look at what she fell onto. Out of the corner of her eye, she spotted a white glint. Acid churned deep within the bowels of her belly, rising ever so steadily up her chest and into her throat. Inch by inch, she turned her head, breathing ragged. Gasping, she crab-crawled away to a clear corner of the pit.

"Shit. Double shit." She covered her nose with her forearm. "Oh god."

It was a wolf, or the remains of one, anyway. There were no signs of life other than the flies buzzing around its carcass. The eyes were hollow and its jaw half eaten. Realizing she had been sitting on a half decayed wolf, with nothing on but her long, black puffer jacket, she scrambled to her feet. She shook in disgust, her ankle crying out under her weight.

"Gross." Her private parts had been flush against the wolf. What if flies crawled up her fuzzy taco? That thought did it, brought the acid from her throat up the rest of the way. Bending over, with one hand on the dirt wall, her stomach clenched and whatever was in it spewed all over the ground. It added yet another smell to her surroundings, wafting up her nose.

"Please let this all be a dream," she begged, puke dribbling down her chin. Staring at the wolf, she wondered if it was the same one that came to her door. Kind of looked like it, but she hadn't gotten a good enough look at it to say for sure.

Maybe it had been a mate or something, and it wanted her to help save it. But it was too late now. The animal had been dead for days. Her heart went out to the creature. No animal deserved to die this way. She didn't deserve to die this way. She refused to let this be the end of her dreams. Looking around, she tried to find a way out.

The pit was about six feet wide and the sides extended high above her head, about another five feet. She was only five-four herself, so that didn't help her situation any. She wanted to get out of there before whoever kidnapped her came back. Did he know about the pit or was it something that previous hunters in the area had built to catch their prey?

Small roots protruded from the dirt walls of the pit. Grabbing onto them, she tried to pull herself up. She got up about three feet up before her hand slipped, making her land on her butt. By the end of all this, she was certain someone would give her the nickname 'rainbow butt.' Not that she was in the habit of flashing her butt at people, but still, the bruises were going to be the entire colour of the rainbow.

Standing up, she ran her hand along the wall. Jenna wondered if the dirt was compact enough to make foot and hand holds. The odd rock jutted out of the wall, which would help give her leverage when needed. Little by little, she inched her way up the wall. Her heart raced as she neared the top. Stretching, she grabbed the edge with one hand, muscles burning under the strain. "I definitely have to work out more."

She reached up with her other hand and grabbed the edge. As she attempted to pull herself up, her foot slipped. "Crap," she cried, as she slid back down the wall, landing next to the wolf. Smacking her hand on the ground, she cried out in frustration. Her ankle ached, and somehow she didn't think her butt was going to be her friend anymore after this. It would probably set up a protest to be moved to a new body.

"Okay, third time's a charm. Right?" She stood up and tried again. Every muscle in her arms and legs shook violently under her weight. "Come on, please." Nearing the top, she reached over the edge, trying to find something secure to hold on to. Her hand brushed against a decent sized tree root popping out of the ground. She wrapped her fingers around it.

"Eureka!"

Gripping it with both hands, she pulled herself up the rest of the way. She had bloody scratches on her arms and legs, but she managed to get out of the hole in the ground. Leaning back against the tree, she laughed, and kept laughing until a twig snapped behind her.

She slapped a hand over her mouth and held her breath. *No. No. No.* Don't let them find her. Not now. Not when this was the furthest she'd been able to get away from the cabin. When she didn't hear any other sound, she twisted slightly to look behind the tree, but didn't spot anything. Another twig snapped from the other side of the tree. She spun the other way and gasped, her hand flying up to her chest.

Letting out a nervous laugh, she dropped her hand to her lap. A brown rabbit. It was just a rabbit. She stood up and tried to remember which direction she had come from. Looking down into the pit, she noticed the wolf was on her side. That meant she crawled up the wrong side. Jenna smacked her forehead. *Great. Just great.*

She tried to go around the pit, but an overgrowth of plant life got in the way. Where was a machete when you needed one? Her legs were now partially numb from the knee-deep snow pressing against her legs. She wasn't sure exactly how much longer she could stay outside. Her hands frozen from the cold roots, fingertips red.

There had to be a way around the pit, but without proper clothes, there was no way she could try to climb over the thick brush. She was also hesitant to return to the cabin to try another route, but what other choice did she have?

Her excitement washed away, like seaweed floating out to sea by the tide. With slumping shoulders, Jenna began her trek back to the cabin. She pushed her way through the bushes when a few branches whipped back in her direction, stinging the sensitive skin on her hand, leaving bright red streaks as a reminder of her current predicament.

"Ouch," she cried, sucking the back of her hand.

As she wandered down the path, she noticed the bushes weren't as thick in one area on her right side, about halfway back to the cabin. Jenna looked down and her heart skipped a beat. There was a fresh footprint in the snow, and it wasn't hers. Someone else was out here with her.

"Just relax. It could be old." She bit the corner of her lip and held her breath, listening to the sounds around her. Birds called in the distance, and the flow of water filled her ears, but other than that, she couldn't hear anything human related.

Tilting her head, she studied the print. One footprint was facing her way, but that was it. They didn't appear to go any further. Instead, whoever it was, turned back around and went back the way they came. Maybe she could follow them and see where they went.

"Bad idea, doofus."

It would lead her straight into the arms of the bad guy. And she wasn't quite ready for an encounter. Her limbs were frozen. She had no choice but to return to the cabin and warm up. Leave the search for another day. She made her way towards the warm building, her limbs stiff and sore. Even her nails had turned a slight blue colour.

They had to be high in the mountains or something because the lower mainland wasn't usually this cold.

Jenna neared the clearing and was about to step out when the sound of snow crunching behind her brought her to a halt. Every muscle in her body taunt. Someone was behind her. His breath warm against her neck.

Her mind said run, but her body froze. *Run. Freeze. Run. Freeze.* She didn't know what to do. And she wasn't sure if her body would listen to her.

Play dead.

That's for bears, you idiot.

Swinging her head back, she connected it with a hard surface. Upon hearing a groan, she took off, running like a mad woman.

Keep running. Don't stop.

She rounded the side of the cabin but was scooped up off her feet, as if she were as light as a feather, and tossed over a shoulder like a sack of potatoes. A hood covered his head, preventing her from seeing his head or his face, but she knew it was a man just by his strength and the width of his shoulders.

"Put me down," she screamed, hitting him on the back. "Someone help me!"

With every scream, the man smacked her on the butt, hard enough for it to sting.

Jenna winced. "Please let me go."

He carried her into the cabin and tossed her on the bed. She crawled off and attempted to run towards the door. The man wrapped his muscular arms around her from behind, trapping her arms under his grip. She stomped on his foot, but it did no good. He must have steel-toed boots on. Pulling her backwards towards the bed, he pulled off her coat.

Completely exposed to the freak, she shrieked and tried to pull away from him. "Stop, please."

Dropping like a dead weight, she tried to slip through his arms, but he tightened his grip and lifted her off the ground. He tossed her back on the bed. Keeping a grip on her left arm, he pulled handcuffs off his belt and cuffed her to the bedpost.

"Please don't do this."

He tilted his head and stared at her, his familiar bright green eyes staring into hers as he handcuffed her other wrist to the post. She knew it. It was him all along. He did this just to get her into bed.

"Let me go, Derek."

CHAPTER ELEVEN

He grinned at her, like she imagined he would, licking his lips as his eyes grazed over the length of her body. She couldn't believe he would put her through all this just so he could get his hands on her. Squirming under his lucid gaze, she used her feet to try to pull the sheets up that he had tossed on the bed with her. He lifted his hand and wagged his finger at her, pulling the sheets right off the bed. She crossed her left leg over her right, trying to hide herself. The guy threw his head back and roared with laughter.

The sound coiled and slithered down her spine. Jenna shivered, breaking out in a cold sweat. This couldn't happen. She didn't want it to happen. It wasn't supposed to go down this way.

When she was ready to settle down, she was going to meet the man of her dreams and get married. He would make love to her on their honeymoon, overlooking the turquoise water of the Caribbean. She wasn't supposed to lose her virginity to some masked freak in a cabin in the middle of nowhere.

The way he stood there, saying nothing, unnerved her.

"I'm not a portrait on the wall, damn it," she snapped, her voice trembling.

He shaped his fingers into a camera and pretended to push a

button, moving around the edges of the bed. A bulge grew in the front of his pants, and even her virgin eyes knew what it meant. Her pulse jumped against the side of her neck.

Looking down, he pointed to his growing member and then to her, making humping motions.

"You're sick," she said, spitting at him.

Again, he wagged his finger and shook his head. Climbing on the bed, he went to straddle her. She kicked him in the side, knocking him off the mattress. He landed with a thud on the hardwood floor. His laughing eyes narrowed, turning cold. Baring his teeth at her, he pulled a rope out of his pocket.

"Just try it," she growled, pulling her legs close to the rest of her body. All ready to go ninja crazy on his ass. "I can't believe you'd do this. I thought you were better than this, Derek."

The masked creep shrugged his shoulders, refusing to utter a word. She'd never known him to be so silent. His mouth was a never ending water fountain, often spewing out liquid gold that women went gaga over. That's why she didn't understand this.

"This may be your fantasy fetish, Derek, but it isn't mine. Let me go, please," she begged.

In a flash, he had her legs in his grip, straddling her backwards. She bucked underneath him but couldn't throw him off. He shimmied his way down her legs until he could tie the rope around her ankles, securing them to the bedposts. By the time he was done, he'd spread her legs wide open.

Standing up, he surveyed his work. She whimpered. Every inch of her body was exposed for his enjoyment. Shivering, Jenna's nipples tightened as her skin contracted and it didn't go unnoticed by the masked man. He stepped towards her.

"No, please," she cried, tugging at the handcuffs that held her wrists. "If you do this, I'll kill you. I swear I'll kill you."

He sat down next to her on the bed and ran his slimy finger between her breasts and down her stomach, stopping just above her bikini line. Bile gathered in the back of her mouth as her stomach muscles quivered under his touch. She tried to twist away from him, but he splayed his hand across her stomach, holding her there.

"If you let me go, I promise I won't tell anyone who you are. Please."

Running his hand back up her body, he caressed her cheek. Jenna bit him on the hand. Growling, he pulled it back and slapped her across the face. Her head whipped to the side under the force of his hand, her jaw joint popping.

"Such a big man, hitting a defenceless woman," she said through clenched teeth, her eyes watering. Patting her on the head, he stood up and walked over to the door.

"You can't seriously be considering leaving me like this," she said. "What if I need to go to the bathroom?"

He didn't acknowledge her. He just opened the door and left.

"Damn you!" she yelled.

A second later, the door slammed open, and he walked in carrying a decent sized blue plastic tote on his shoulder. Her breathing quickened as he neared the bed. She didn't want to know what was in the tote. It couldn't be anything good. But it had to be better than what she thought he was going to do.

Jenna changed her mind as soon as he opened the tote and turned it upside down, dumping the contents on her naked body. Screaming, she pulled at the ropes and handcuffs, desperate to break free.

"You can't leave me all alone. Not now!" Iris clung to her husband, crying.

Daniel pulled her into his arms and held her close. "I have to go."

"I can't do this on my own."

"Work won't wait for our lives to get back to normal. If you want to keep this roof over your head, I have to go back."

She pushed him away and said, "Our daughter is gone. Lost. She might even be dead, and all you care about is money."

It's not that he cared about the money, but if he spent any more time twiddling his thumbs, he'd go crazy. He was liable to lose it on his already distraught wife. Iris was at her wit's end, and it seemed like all she ever did was cry. Her eyes were constantly puffy and red.

As for him, he wanted to hit something. Break something. Release all the pent up energy someway somehow. It didn't help that the sexual tension was building inside him, too. He couldn't even be close to his wife because it was the last thing on her mind. Work was the only option to get his mind off everything.

Iris' mind was too busy for him, and as for her body, the train's tunnel shut down ages ago. They lived together and yet it felt like they were a million miles apart. "Why do you care whether I stay or go?"

"I need you."

"For what? "

Iris opened her mouth, then snapped it closed. What could she say? She knew that if she tried to make him stay, he'd be miserable, and in the end, she'd feel like crap for pushing him. The last thing she wanted to do was jeopardize their shaky relationship and have him say the most dreaded word in a marriage. *Divorce.*

That wasn't something she could handle right now. They'd been on the verge of it once before when they lost Rebecca, their other daughter. They'd tried for so long to have kids, spent thousands on fertility meds, only for reality to give them a deathly blow.

"I need your strength right now," she said, pressing her forehead against his chest.

"It is only for a few days. I'll call you every night."

He wouldn't call her. He never did, but she nodded her head, anyway. Sadness pooled deep in her belly. They were hanging on by a thread, and the newest trial would likely be the one that broke it.

"Love you, babe." He planted a kiss on her lips, picked up his suit-case, and walked out the door. Daniel didn't look back, not even when he got into the car. Was it that hard to acknowledge her? Was she really that unlovable?

Iris wrapped her arms around herself as she watched her

husband drive away, wondering if this might be the time he keeps going and never comes home. She half expected it, especially once Jenna grew up.

"Jenna, where are you?" she whispered, her voice disappearing into the wind swirling around her. How could life be so cruel as to strip another child away from her? If she lost both her daughter and her husband, she wouldn't want to go on living.

Life would have no meaning for her anymore. Her parents were gone. The rest of her siblings were halfway across the world. Her oldest child was buried in the ground, and her youngest, Jenna...

A loud sob broke free as she pushed the door closed. Leaning against the door, she slid down to the floor. "God, please don't let me lose my family. Can't I have just one miracle in my life?"

After a few minutes, she stood up and walked into her bedroom. She pulled open the top drawer of her white two-drawer bedside table, pulling out a picture that had been hidden in the back for years. Wiping off a thin layer of dust, she stared at the infants in the photo. Rebecca was sitting in her car seat, wearing a white and pink sleeper. Her sister, Jenna, was sound asleep in the seat beside her, but not Rebecca. She was wide awake and as curious as could be.

Tears slid down Iris' face. The twins had been born prematurely, and she had waited months to take them home. It was the most amazing and terrifying day of her life. She didn't know what she was doing or how she was going to handle them both, but she was so ecstatic to break them out of their hospital jail.

But it was never meant to be. One survived. The other...Iris shook her head. The pain was just too much. And now, it was like it was that same day all over again. Different circumstances, but the end result might very well be the same.

Darn it! Parents weren't supposed to bury their own children. The concept was backwards. Inside out. Whatever. It was the total opposite of what it should be. They were supposed to live to a good old age, even push her around in a wheelchair when she was finally too old to walk for herself.

She wanted grandkids, wanted to be able to spoil them with

candy before bedtime. Slip them money when their parents weren't looking. Walk with them through the forest, taking the time to stop and look at every bug. Every flower. Treasuring every single second life blessed them with.

She'd wasted so much of her time on stupid things, worrying about things that, in the end, never really mattered. She let the precious moments in her kid's life pass her by because she was too caught up in her mind to notice the seconds ticking by. Seconds she could no longer take back.

Why did people only realize things like this when it was too late? Placing the photo back in the drawer, she curled into a ball on the bed, letting the tears fall. All she wanted for Christmas was her baby back. Nothing else mattered.

Was she doomed to lose everyone she loved? It certainly felt like it. A dark cloud descended over her mind, overshadowing any ray of light that she desperately tried to hold onto.

"Oh, Jenna," she murmured. "Please come home."

CHAPTER TWELVE

"You bastard. Get them off me!" She tried hard not to shiver as the snakes slithered across her skin. Their muscles rippled down the length of their body as they moved, like a rock having been thrown into a pond. The scales on their belly dug into her skin to gain traction.

Against her own volition, her stomach contracted under their movement. She had no idea whether they were venomous, and she really didn't want to find out. "Please, get them off me," she cried, tears forming in her eyes.

Her heart thumped against her chest, her breath came in short raspy gasps. She was afraid that if she took a deep breath, they might bite her. She had no idea what they were, only that they were a pale yellow colour, with blotches of brown. And there appeared to be a number of them, all at least three feet long. Their fork-like tongues darted continuously in and out of their mouths. She jumped each time one touched her skin.

One slithered up towards her face. Jenna squeezed her eyes closed. *It's not real. It's not real.* This is all in her imagination. Oh, hell, who was she kidding? The snake moved under her arm and wrapped itself around it. The masked man leaned down to pick up a snake that had fallen to the floor, but must have thought better of it when it reared up and hissed at him. He backed away and watched the show.

A tickle grew in the back of her throat as a snake's tail slid across her nostrils and mouth. She pressed her lips closed and tried not to breathe. *Please don't sneeze.* A scale caught on the corner of her dry lips, ripping off a piece of dead skin. She grunted in pain.

The tickle intensified, and the sensation spread into her eyes. It was coming whether she wanted it to or not. She tried to swallow the sneeze, and her body jerked in the process, upsetting the already disturbed snakes. The reptile on her chest lashed out, biting her on the upper arm, hissing. She cried out in pain as it sunk its fangs into her skin. Her kidnapper clapped his hands gleefully and grinned.

"Don't just stand there, do something," she cried, her body shaking. Instead of helping, the man just walked out the door, humming a tune. He shut the door behind him, leaving her behind, with the creatures crawling all over her naked body.

Her arm burned, and she swore she could feel the venom trickling into her blood. "Damn you," she yelled, but then zipped her lips closed when a snake hissed at her. Tears flowed down her cheeks, dampening the pillow beneath her head.

She swallowed hard as she looked at the bloody bite on her arm, half expecting to see two fang marks, but instead it looked like two U's on her arm, one inside the other.

"Please, don't let me die," she whispered as she stared at the ceiling. Not wanting to get bit again, she lay on the bed as still as possible. Her chest ached with each breath. With only one bite, she hoped she would have a fighting chance.

One snake slithered across her throat, leaving her gasping for air under its weight. There was nothing she could do. Her hands were tied, literally. She couldn't move, shift, or do anything other than wait. And she didn't know what she was waiting for. Life? Death? Gangrene?

Even if the snakes weren't poisonous, they could give her one heck of an infection. She was thankful he didn't use spiders. She hated snakes, but spiders gave her the heebie jeebies.

When she was younger, she'd gone out to the garage to throw something in the garbage and when she opened the lid, there sat a huge honkin' spider. It freaked her out so much that spiders became her number one enemy. They were both equally dangerous, but maybe it had something to do with her picking up garter snakes when she was a kid. They made the whole snake world a little less scary, but these didn't look like the garter snakes she remembered.

Okay. She was rambling now. Was that what people did when they were on the verge of death? Or maybe it was just before people went psycho. No, she wasn't crazy. The man who put her here was the very definition of psycho.

As she lay there, still as a statue, the reptiles eventually made their way to the floor, giving her room to breathe. If she lived to see the sun rise one more day, she couldn't help but wonder what the masked man had in store for her next. After this, she wasn't sure she even wanted to find out.

Johnathan stepped into the bar. The very same one Jenna disappeared from a week earlier. He knew that after forty-eight hours the chance of finding a missing person alive decreased considerably, but he refused to give up.

Tonight, he was going to follow up on the only lead he had so far. Squinting, he surveyed the patrons and spotted his old partner sitting on a bar stool at the counter, wearing his signature black suit. Squeezing his way through the crowds on the dance floor, he sat on the empty stool next to him.

"Hi, Phillip."

"Johnathan."

"You said you weren't going to come back here."

"I have my reasons," he said, signalling the bartender to drop another shot of whiskey.

"Anything to do with Maria?"

The man's hand shook as he brought the glass up to his lips. Tilting his head back, he downed the shot. "I'm close, man."

"Is that what you've been doing all these years?" John asked, studying his old friend. Dark, saggy bags framed Phillip's sunken eyes and his clothes hung off his body. Evidence that the passing years weren't exactly favourable to him, but he didn't look like he cared.

"When was the last time you had a good meal?" he asked Phillip. His friend shrugged his shoulders and stared into the empty glass. "Okay, that settles it. You are coming to our house for dinner."

"I can't. I need to stay here."

"You aren't doing yourself any good if you are dead on your feet. Come on."

The man groaned, but he allowed John to grab him by the jacket, pulling him towards the door. Phillip had saved his butt on more than one occasion, and he wasn't about to watch him waste away. Not if there was something he could do to help.

"When did you get into town?" John asked.

"A few weeks back."

"And you didn't call me?"

His friend shrugged his shoulders again. "After what happened…"

"None of that was your fault."

"I shot you."

John looked at him over the roof of the car. His friend's eyes were still full of guilt. "Who doesn't get shot in our line of work?"

Phillip shook his head and ducked into the vehicle. "You're crazy, dude."

"Maybe so." John really didn't know who the man was next to him anymore, but he was in the business of saving lives, and Phillip looked like he needed saving this time. He owed the man his life on more than one occasion, and it was the least he could do. "Jodi is making her infamous meatloaf."

"What made you call me?" the man asked.

"We can talk about that later. For now, let's have some chow."

In truth, he was hesitant to bring it up. His friend looked slightly unhinged and off-balance. Maybe, he would be more himself once he had a belly full of food instead of just liquor.

"Sounds good," Phillip said.

Back at the house, it wasn't long before their bellies were overflowing, and they were inside his study with the door closed. Phillip was standing next to the fireplace mantel, looking at a picture of the two of them in their uniform, taken when they first became partners.

"I can't believe you still have this picture."

"Two gung-ho youngsters."

Phillip laughed. "That we were."

"I was surprised that we weren't stripped of our weapons in our first year."

"We did get knocked up the side of the head by the Captain, though."

Johnathan poured two glasses of whiskey and sat down, propping his feet up on his desk. Phillip took a seat on the couch opposite his desk, staring at the liquid in the glass. They sat in silence for a few moments, each caught up in their own memories. Some darker than others.

It was strange seeing his old partner after all these years. To be honest, he was surprised Phillip even answered the phone and agreed to meet with him. The man had totally dropped off the radar and refused to have anything to do with the precinct or even him anymore, even though they had been police academy buddies.

"There were rumours that you'd gone rogue. Is that why you left?" John asked.

"The captain wanted to close the file on my wife. I couldn't do that."

"You've been trying to find her killer?"

Phillip looked down at the carpet, nodding his head.

"Is that why you were at the library last week?"

His head shot up, eyes wide. "How'd you know?"

"Someone saw you talking with Jenna McCay after the fire."

Phillip stood up and walked over to the office window and looked out over the garden. "She saved my life, such a sweet thing."

Taking a sip of his whiskey, John swished it around in his mouth before swallowing. "They said she found you in the janitor's closet? A very unusual spot to be if you don't work there."

"Yep."

He was certainly being tight-lipped about it, and that didn't sit well with John. Somehow he had a feeling this had to do with his ex-partner's wife. "How'd you wind up in there?"

"Looking for evidence."

That piqued his interest. "Why would evidence be in there?"

Phillip turned around to face him and leaned against the wall, stuffing his hands in his pockets. "I've been following a man around for the last few months, Craig Stevenson. He's the evening janitor at the library."

John dropped his feet to the floor and leaned on the desk with his forearms. "He's the one guy we haven't found to interview yet."

"Well, Detective, hunt him down. I'm certain he knows about the missing persons."

"We'll send out an APB. Come on, let's have one more drink."

CHAPTER THIRTEEN

Jenna was braver than he gave her credit for. The other women totally lost it when he'd brought the snakes out. Once she got over the initial shock and the bite, she didn't really pay them any attention, seemed more interested in breaking free.

He had a feeling it wouldn't take her long to realize that if she could make her limbs stretch far enough, the cuffs could actually slide up and over the bedposts. As he watched her on the screen, his right eye began to sting. Squeezing it closed, he stood up and made his way to the washroom.

It actually surprised him that he could keep the contacts in for so long. He'd never worn them before. Glasses were much less of a hassle and never stung his eyes or made him want to poke out his eyeballs. He couldn't understand why anyone would wear contacts on a daily basis.

Today, though, it was all for show. A part of the game. He actually couldn't wait to ramp things up a little. Phase two had been thoroughly enjoyable so far. The hunt—the chase—had been incredibly arousing. He had a few more things in mind before moving onto the next round.

In a few hours, he'd go back in and grab the snakes, then play around with her a little more. He could bet she had never seen a naked man in real life, let alone have one do things to her.

That was always his favourite part of the game. He always laughed whenever they would fight against him and not want to orgasm, but he could always make them, much to their anger and frustration.

Walking over to the fridge, he pulled out a beer and returned to watch her on the screen. Jenna was perfect. Her breasts were perky, and she had a little meat on her bones. Nothing like the skinny underweight models on magazine covers. Ones that looked they hadn't eaten a decent meal in months.

Her curves were mouth-watering, and he wanted to taste every inch of them. He would have to make sure she was completely secure, more than she was at the moment, or he'd be sporting a groin injury.

When she started working at the library, she caught his attention right away. Well, she caught the attention of nearly every guy working there. Not that she showed any interest in anyone. She was too busy dreaming about traveling.

"You are going to give me all the attention I want now," he murmured to the screen.

He would be seared into her memory forever for as long as she lived. And who knows, maybe she'd be the first person to survive his game. Young people often bounced back the quickest.

She was nineteen-years-old, which was a year in his own life he could no longer remember. It was tucked away in the far recesses of his mind. He figured that was the year they had locked him up in the psych ward after his mom passed away. His family claimed he was going to hurt himself.

The year was a total blur. But he stumbled his way through and eventually obtained his medical degrees. His specialty was the human mind, but again, his sanity was questioned with the experiments he wanted to conduct, so he disappeared off the radar.

Mathew Graham ceased to exist in that moment, in the eyes of the world, anyway. He faked his death, took on another name, and started a new life on the coast. Working in a library was not exactly his dream job, but it was a means to an end. This—what he was doing here—was exactly what he wanted to do. Test the limits and reach past the boundaries. Ones that normal people weren't allowed to cross.

On his own, he didn't have to hear how much of a disappointment he was. Something his dad had reminded him of constantly. Weak is what he said. And he never failed to let him know he would never amount to anything in his life.

His mom had been his rock. His dad, quicksand. He was the one that put him in the hospital, under the guise of 'my kid is psycho.' He just didn't want the responsibility of caring for him and had wanted him out of the house.

Walking over to the dartboard, he grabbed a few darts and moved about ten feet away. Square in the middle of the bullseye was a picture of his father, with multiple holes in the glossy paper. Throwing a dart at the picture, he said, "I hate you, Dad."

"Crap, I gotta pee." Jenna glanced around the room. The snakes had settled in front of the fireplace on the opposite side of the room. No longer moving. She tugged at her left wrist and then her right.

Grunting, she gave her wrist a good yank, but it didn't budge. Looking down at her feet, she jiggled her foot. The ropes were tied securely to her ankles but appeared to be fairly loose on the posts. She had to get free before he came back and before she peed the bed.

As she moved her leg, the rope moved up and down the post. Biting on the corner of her lip, she remembered doing a bridge in gymnastics when she was younger. Maybe, if she could arch her body enough, she could throw her leg high enough into the air and the rope would slip over the top of the post.

Placing her hands behind her head, she arched her back and threw her left leg into the air. The first attempt failed, and Jenna fell back against the sheets, cursing herself for being so short.

"Damn it!"

Was the man watching her? She could bet he was, considering there was a microphone and speaker hidden somewhere in the room. That made her even more self-conscious as embarrassment stirred inside her. Determined to get free, she arched into the air again, throwing her leg up the post.

The rope approached the top, but didn't go over. Her skin burned against the coarse material with each attempt. If there was one thing she was happy with, it was that her parents blessed her with a stubborn 'never give up' attitude. It got her into trouble now and then, and they always lectured her about focusing her stubbornness in the right direction. Tonight, she was glad it was part of her personality.

"Come on, stubbornness. Don't fail me now." She kicked her leg again, and this time the rope flew over the top. Falling back against the bed, she laughed nervously. *One down, three to go.*

Now that she had more movement, it was much easier to get the other rope up and over, leaving the bottom half of her body free. Looking at the snakes, she was relieved to see they hadn't budged at all.

Her bladder was ready to burst, and the pressure between her legs intensified. With her legs free, she pulled herself to a sitting position at the head of the bed and worked her handcuffs up the bedposts. In no time at all, she was free.

Standing up, she ran to the washroom, making it to the toilet just in time. Her quick movements alerted the snakes, and they stirred. Jenna slammed the door closed with her foot. One bite was enough for her.

As she sat there doing her business, she examined her arm. The pain had died down a little and her skin wasn't doing anything funky around the bite. If the snakes were venomous, she was certain she'd feel something by now. Not that she was a doctor or anything.

When she was done, Jenna poked her head out of the bathroom and was happy to see the snakes in the same spot as before. She tiptoed to the front door and attempted to open it.

"Damn."

He'd locked it again. Seriously, didn't he already have the place surrounded with traps? What was the point of locking the door? She wanted to kick and scream, but chose against it. She didn't feel like playing *Ring Around the Rosie* with a bunch of snakes. Playing that game with kids at school had been annoying enough.

But damn. She really wanted the door to still be unlocked. She had hoped by opening the door, the snakes would wander outside. It was cold and snakes hated the cold, but it was worth a try. It's not like she could flush them down the toilet.

Smacking herself on the forehead, Jenna stopped in front of the window and pushed it open. It was like a light bulb going off over her head. She might not be able to climb out because of the bars, but the nasty critters could fit through them.

If she grabbed them near their heads and used the broom handle to lift their bodies, she should be able to pick them up without getting bitten. *But* she'd probably get bit trying to let them go. She groaned. That was not something she wanted to chance, but what other choice did she have? It was them or her.

The man had left the tote on the ground. Maybe she could toss it on top of them and slide the lid underneath. They were all in a heap in front of the fireplace. If she moved slowly, she should be able to trap them. Jenna glanced around the room with apprehension. The masked freak was probably watching her and laughing.

Creep.

Grabbing her jacket, she slipped it on. The fire in the fireplace was dying, and the room was getting cold again, but she couldn't put any logs on the fire with the snakes in the way.

Praying and hoping that the box would fit over all of them, she picked it up and side-stepped her way towards the reptiles, bare feet and all. If it didn't work, nothing would save her toes from becoming a meal.

Holding her breath, she lowered the tote.

CHAPTER FOURTEEN

When the container was a foot above the resting reptiles, she dropped it over them, accidentally catching the tail of a snake on the edge of the tote. The snake tried to wiggle its way out.

She shoved it back under the box before the space allowed others to crawl out. Giddy with success, she sat on top of the box to hold it in place as it bounced back and forth under the force of their breakout attempts. Glancing around the room, she spotted the lid near the bed. And her newfound excitement dimmed.

Smacking the tote, she said, "Great! Now what?" She really didn't think this one through. "Damn it!"

Now she had a bunch of angry snakes, and if she moved, they would probably launch the container like a rocket across the room. Even her phone was sitting on the kitchen table, which was too far away for her to reach. If she had it, she could at least read something while she waited for them to settle.

Crossing her legs, she sat there and rested her chin on her hand. This was going to make for a super long day. Why had her life suddenly gone to hell the moment she turned nineteen? It was like it was just waiting for her to get over her teen years before bowling her over and sending her into her own personal hell hole.

"This isn't supposed to happen to me," she yelled. "Do you hear me?"

Silence.

"I know you're listening to me, you creep. Let me out of here." The more she yelled, the more rambunctious the reptiles became, but the man involved didn't respond. What outcome did she expect from her outburst? It's not like he was going to come running to her rescue. If he came, he'd probably shut her up by sending something else nasty her way.

She sat there, drumming her cheek with her fingers as she waited. For what exactly, she didn't know. "I want my clothes back," she yelled again. Her jacket didn't cut it, not against the cool winter air seeping into the cabin.

"What do you want from me?" she cried.

The snakes hit the box again, almost knocking it over. She placed her feet on the ground to keep her balance. "Stop it," she said, banging the box. That made them hiss and bang again.

Quiet, you moron.

If she kept quiet, they might settle down long enough for her to get up and finish what she started. The last thing she wanted was to spend the rest of her life in this crappy place, being the creep's play thing.

She couldn't say exactly how long she sat there for, but, finally, the animals calmed down. They weren't hitting the sides of the container anymore. Did she dare get up, though? What if her movements alerted them? Why couldn't she be a featherweight?

Resting her hands on her knees, Jenna slowly stood up, praying she wouldn't disturb the slimy slithering beasts. The tote bounced again, so she quickly sat back down. "Come on, you dickheads, play nice."

They were getting on her nerves. She should have just started whacking them with a chair or used the chair legs as stakes instead of this brilliant idea. Growling, she picked up the magazine on the coffee table and hurled it across the room.

"Shoot." She should have used the magazine to pass the time

instead of throwing it away. She could have made paper airplanes or read the articles inside. "Impulsive meathead!"

There were only so many ways a person could entertain themselves sitting in one spot. Play finger puppets on the wall. See how many shapes she could make with her fingers. Count the knots on the hardwood floors or the goose bumps on her legs.

"Jeez, it's getting cold."

The snakes had finally settled down, and so she tried to stand up again. This time, it seemed to work. They didn't budge and remained calm. Walking on her tiptoes, she silently headed towards the lid.

As she approached the side of the couch, she saw some movement out of the corner of her eye. Jenna shrieked and ran to the kitchen, jumping on a chair. The sound alerted the snakes, and the tote fell over, freeing them.

She climbed onto the kitchen table, pulling her knees to her chest, staring at the new intruders and the old ones. "Just when you think it can't get any worse."

The floor behind the couch was littered with live disease-ridden rats. Where the heck did they come from? How'd he get them into the room without her seeing him? She was sitting right there. It wasn't like he just waltzed in the door and dropped them without her knowledge.

There was no way she was coming down off the chair. The floor belonged to the animal kingdom now. They could duke it out all they wanted and leave her out of it. The chair and table, those were her territory.

If any of them tried to come over to her, she'd...she'd...heck, she had no idea what she'd do. It wasn't like she had a weapon of any sort. Salt and pepper shakers were on the table, but it's not like the critters were slugs and would shrivel up and die if she dumped salt on them.

Maybe the snakes would eat the rats and the problem would solve itself. How many rats could one snake eat during a sitting? If only she'd paid more attention to the nature channel instead of cramming her head full of crap, she might actually have an answer.

It didn't take long before one snake caught the whiff of a rat and struck out at it, catching it between its powerful jaws. The rodent didn't even know what hit him. That sparked an all-out war between the two species. Both battling for dominance while she watched from her perch on the chair.

Jenna hadn't realized that rats were formidable foes, but as she watched one go to town on a snake, she realized the fight wouldn't be over as quickly as she had thought or hoped.

"Kill them, you lousy reptiles!" she yelled before slapping her hands over her mouth. Drawing attention to herself would not be a good thing. She didn't want them to forget about doing themselves in. Unfortunately, the snakes were outnumbered, and that didn't bode well for their survival.

A few of the rodents ran up the curtain and out the window, while others kept battling it out with the snakes. The numbers on both teams dwindled, and soon only two snakes were left and a handful of rats.

At least that kind of helped her problem, but not completely. The two species were staring at each other from opposite sides of the room where they had retreated to nurse their wounds.

She had to wonder what other animals the masked creep planned to spring on her. And how the heck did he get the rats into the room without her seeing him? Was there a trapdoor or something she didn't know about? Curious, she stepped off the chair and jumped onto the couch.

Leaning over the back, she examined the floor. There didn't appear to be anything that she could see. Scratching her head, she looked around. How the heck did he do it? If she could find out, that might just be her ticket out of the cabin.

One thing at a time, though. She had to figure out the rest of her rodent and reptile problem. They partially solved it for her, for which she was grateful. All she had to do now was figure out how to get the rest of them out of the cabin.

"I bet you think you're a hoot," she said, sticking her tongue out at the unseen, masked villain.

～

He certainly thought so. His plan had worked perfectly. Soon, she would find the hidden tunnel and the next round of his games would begin. The maze funhouse was a great spot for playing cat and mouse. The torture rooms she'd run into trying to get away were some of his favourite places.

Thanks to his genius IQ, he managed to get enough money to create his little house of horrors. The best part of all was that he was too smart to get caught. He had embezzled millions from just a quick keystroke on his keyboard.

He chuckled when she leaned over the back of the sofa. She was so bloody close to finding one of his hidden trapdoors. He couldn't believe how incredibly bright she was for someone so young, so inquisitive. Curiosity did kill the cat though, so he'd have to be careful.

The more he learned about her, the more he wondered whether he wanted to push her as far as the others. Marriage kept seeping into his mind instead. He couldn't help but wonder whether anyone has ever got married over the phone? He'd have to look into it.

Yes.

That's exactly what he wanted to do. She wasn't going to like the idea, but that didn't bother him any. He loved women with a little fight in them. The young ones had more spunk, more energy than the older women did. He'd finally have someone who could keep up with him. And he wouldn't be lonely anymore.

Blah.

He was getting ahead of himself. This wasn't about finding a woman. He had to keep his mind on the task. His work was more important. He couldn't let himself get distracted.

Shit.

He gripped the back of his neck. What the heck was happening to him?

CHAPTER FIFTEEN

"Hi, Ms. Hampton," Detective Charleston said. "Can I get you anything to drink?"

"Not unless you want me running to the bathroom before we're done."

John cleared his throat and took a seat at his desk. He could see why most of the employees were intimidated by her. "Okay, I guess we'll get started then. What can you tell me about Craig Stevenson?"

"Cute butt?" she said, smirking. "He had the type that you just wanted to pinch when he walked by. You've got one, too, by the way."

Blood rushed to his face, and he cleared his throat again. He wasn't interested in talking about his ass. "What type of person was he?"

"Oh, he's very charming. He even took me out to dinner once."

He wanted to roll his eyes and smack her up the side of the head to knock some focus into her. It would make his job a little easier if she could stay on task. "Did he miss a lot of work?"

"Not to my knowledge, but then again, I don't have time to henpeck everyone."

"Just Jenna?"

"Officer, if you ask me, that girl is trouble. She's a walking disaster," the woman said as she tried to smooth out her wrinkled skirt.

He tilted his head. "Why do you say that?"

"I've never met anyone so accident prone. She's been a huge distraction for the rest of my team. They are always cleaning up her messes."

"You don't like her?"

Ms. Hampton pursed her lips, crossing her arms over her hefty bosom.

"I'll take that as a no." Could she be involved in Jenna's disappearance? He didn't like the vibe he was getting from her. "Do you know what may have happened to her?"

She turned to stare out the window, appearing to be lost in thought.

"Ms. Hampton?"

"What?" she snapped, tears glistening in her eyes.

He held out a box of tissues to the old woman. There was a story behind her tears, and it wasn't about Jenna's disappearance. "Are you okay?"

"I'm fine," she replied, snatching a tissue from the box. "Can I go now?"

He doubted she had any information that would be useful to the case, but he had to try. "Is there anything you can tell me that might help us solve this case? Do you know if Craig has any other property in the area?"

"I only know of the address he has on file."

"When was the last time you saw him?"

"The night of the storm."

Detective Charleston's eyes widened, and he leaned forward. "He was at the library?"

If he was, Craig was the only person who never gave a statement about what happened. The firefighters told him everyone had been evacuated out of the building. Where did the man go? Why didn't he stick around to be questioned?

"Have you heard from him since then?"

"No."

Great. Another missing person's case to be solved, but he had a strange vibe about this particular one. He'd have to send an agent over to the man's house. "If you can think of anything that might help us, please call and let me know."

"Bye, Detective Charleston."

Using the arm rests as leverage, Ms. Hampton stood up slowly, her hip cracking. The woman was beyond retirement age, but she kept right on working. He surmised it was to keep her mind busy so she couldn't think about her regrets. She seemed to carry a lot of them, if the pain in her eyes was any indication.

John got up and escorted her out to a grey station wagon in the parking lot. The car was a rust bucket, with scratches up and down the sides and a dent in the rear left bumper. She sure wasn't one for vehicle upkeep.

"Have a good day, Ms. Hampton."

Scowling, she slammed the door, nearly catching his fingers. He couldn't help but wonder what flew up her craw and made her the epitome of the crazy old cat lady. She was fine at the beginning of their conversation, but then she turned increasingly cold when the conversation turned to Jenna.

Ms. Hampton wasn't too forthcoming with information, so he would have to have to dig a little deeper. Dig into her past and see if there were any connections to Craig. Detective Charleston typed the man's name into the database and came up with one hit. The man had a squeaky clean record. As he wrote the man's address on a sticky note, he noticed that the section for the next of kin was empty.

"That's odd." No emergency contact to call if a serious illness struck him.

Pulling up the man's birth certificate, he noted the names of his parents and added a sticky note to the file to contact them first thing in the morning. Johnathan's instincts told him it was a fake ID and if it was, Craig knew how to plant false information into even the most secure government databases on the planet.

They could be dealing with an entirely different level of criminal activity here. Someone who had an inside track on how their systems worked. If that was the case, the guy would always be one step ahead of the game because he'd know exactly what was going on.

He'd have to talk with Phillip again and get his intel on the guy. John was pretty certain that his ex-partner knew more than he was letting on. Turning off his computer, he stared out the window. Snow was falling yet again. It made him thankful to have a nice, warm house to go home to, as that hadn't always been the case. Hopefully, Jenna was somewhere warm, alive, and kicking.

Hope was hard to have in his line of work, especially after all the evil he had seen over the years, but he had to hold on to whatever strands of hope he had left. Otherwise, he'd become as bitter as the families he'd dealt with in his career. That's why Johnathan stayed, to be that hope for others. He'd stay until no other option remained.

"I should probably call Iris," Daniel said to himself as he laid his head on the pillow.

But he didn't want to disrupt the peaceful waves crashing against the seashore of Long Beach. There was a calmness about it you couldn't find in the city. Surrey might be known as the city of parks, but it was growing rapidly, and skyscrapers were littering the skyline now. He preferred these small out of the way places on Vancouver Island.

They were going to buy a place down in White Rock to be closer to the beach, but property was too expensive, so they had settled in an area that left much to be desired, as opposed to the sweet beach house he had his heart set on.

Given their current income status, they could probably afford it now, but what was the point? They had no more kids to raise and at the rate they were going, they would have no relationship to enter into retirement with either.

Iris kept getting trapped in her own mind and didn't seem to care about what the rest of them were going through. Here, he could breathe and just worry about his own issues instead of hers. Problems, that no matter how hard he tried, he couldn't fix them, and that irritated him to no end.

Laying there, with his forearm covering his eyes, he wished for an easier life. One not marred with challenges and defeats. His daughter had been gone a week, and no one had any answers on her whereabouts.

If he hadn't returned to work, he'd be out there tearing the city upside down looking for Jenna, wringing the neck of the man who should have been watching out for her. Derek should have gone after her and made sure she got home safe. What kind of man lets a young woman go off on their own in an unsavoury part of town?

The same type of man who leaves his wife alone when she needs him.

"Shut up," he growled.

His conscience was right, though. That was the whole reason he avoided calling her. Hearing her voice would make him feel even guiltier than he did already. In an attempt to get his mind off of her and the situation, he almost did the unmentionable. He'd been close to inviting his assistant into the room with him.

Christy was more than eager to become something more and wasn't afraid to let him know it. She knew all about the struggles in his life and didn't mind hearing him rant about it. He was starving sexually, and his wife couldn't see it, but this woman could.

But he couldn't do it, couldn't hurt his wife, no matter what he was struggling with himself. He made a vow to her and intended to keep it. Rolling over, he picked up his phone up off the nightstand. He jumped when it rang in his hand.

"Hello?" he answered.

"You said you'd call me."

"I was actually just about to —"

"Don't. Just don't," Iris said, her voice rising an octave.

"Sorry," he said, sighing.

"When are you coming home?"

"As soon as I can. Have you heard anything?" he asked, running his hand down his face.

"That's why I'm calling. I just spoke with Detective Charleston. He thinks he might have a lead."

Daniel sat up in bed, swinging his legs over the side. "What? Who?"

"I don't know, but he's following up on it tomorrow and told us to stick close to the phones."

That picked up his spirits. "I'll be on the first flight out."

"Are you sure? Doesn't the conference last another day or two?"

"They can do without me. If he's about to find our daughter, I want to be there."

Just then, Christy walked in with her thin silky nightgown and mouthed, "who is it?"

"My wife," he answered, looking away from her. He knew when to flee temptation. This trip had been a bad idea from the start, and if he didn't leave now, he couldn't say what would happen. He didn't want to cheat, but his body was not in line with his mind when Christy looked like that.

"Are you really going to come home tomorrow?" Iris asked.

"Yes."

His wife stayed silent on the other end, and he sensed that she didn't believe him. And who could blame her. He hadn't really been a man of his word over the last few years.

"Promise?"

"I promise!"

CHAPTER SIXTEEN

Two days later, Jenna was still pleased with herself for ridding the house of the remaining pests. But she wasn't quite sure whether she was happy or perturbed that the creep had left her alone since then. She'd been hoping he'd come and unlock the door again. She didn't like the feeling of being a sitting duck, especially knowing what the guy was like.

Was he going to surprise her in the middle of the night? Did he have cameras in the house? Was he watching her right now? She zipped up her jacket and wrapped her arms around herself, cuddling deep under the covers on the couch.

Evening had fallen. The lucent moon was casting its shadow on the walls of the cabin, like ghosts dancing in the night. The flames in the fireplace flickered with their own ceremonious dance. She leaned her head against the armrest of the couch and stared at the flames.

As she dozed off, a loud, screeching cry pierced the night air. Jenna gasped and jumped off the couch, pressing her back against the wall farthest from the noise. Her heart skipped a beat as she held her breath, not wanting to make a sound.

The hair-raising, baby-like cry filled the air again, sounding like it was right next to her. She crouched to the ground, covering her ears, but it made no difference. The sound vibrated off her eardrums, making her cringe.

Kneeling, she poked the top of her head over the windowsill to see what was outside. When a dark figure rushed by, she ducked. Her heart was ready to jump out of her chest, her breathing ragged. It moved so fast, she couldn't even see the shape.

Whatever it was kept circling the cabin, occasionally scratching at the exterior paneling. She had to get out of here. There were no ifs, ands or buts about it. If her abductor could get in here, without coming in through the front door, she could get out. The last thing she was going to do was wait around and become that thing's lunch.

She had tried to find the hidden door before, but so far had no luck uncovering it. However, this time, she wouldn't give up until she found it. It was somewhere. She knew it was. Crawling along the floor, she ran her fingers along the wooden floorboards, looking for small gaps between them. The light in the cabin didn't help matters much. Three-quarters of the boards hid in the shadows.

Tapping the ground, she listened for changes in the sounds echoing back at her. As she moved behind the couch and tapped again, she heard a different pitch than before. It sounded hollow. As she continued her search, she came across a slight ridge in the wood, about two feet long.

Jenna tried to pry it open with her fingers but could not get enough of a grip to lift it. The only way to get it open would be to find something skinny and shove it through the micro-opening. Rummaging through the drawers and cupboards, she found a butter knife. "Please, let it work."

As she slid the knife between the boards, she prayed nothing sinister or evil was waiting for her down there. She wished she had a normal flashlight to use, but there was nothing to light the way, except for her phone.

Images of eight-legged freaks appeared in her mind, and worry rattled her to her core. She didn't want to run into any mutated spiders that could swallow you whole or light you on fire.

"Where do you think you are, Jenna? Trapped in the Lavalantula movie?" she mumbled.

She may be living in her own personal horror movie, but the world still had some basic unbroken laws. There were no spiders the size of motorhomes. No three headed sharks that could ride around in tornadoes. It was just her and the deranged freak of a man. And the thing that was hunting her outside.

When she finally opened the trapdoor, she glanced down into the darkness. A faint light illuminated the pathway below. Placing her phone in her pocket, she took a deep breath and then stepped onto the first rung of the ladder.

The cool metal stung her fingers as she made her way down. She left the trapdoor wide open in case she had to make a hasty retreat. The moment her foot hit the dirt floor, she knew she was in way over her head. Human skulls lined the walls, tucked away in their own little alcoves.

Spider webs branched out in orb-like patterns across the ceiling, but in the dim light, she couldn't see where the residents of the webs were hiding. That made it even more eerie. Jenna's legs shook, and she sucked in a breath as she walked down the unknown haunted hallway.

"I should have brought the broom handle."

It wasn't too late to be smart and not be like the unprepared ninny who decided to open the door when a murderer was standing outside.

She quickly scrambled back up the ladder, grabbed the broom, and then climbed her way back down into the tunnel. Taking a deep breath, she began her trek down the musty hall. A mouse scurried between her feet, quickly disappearing into a hole. She jumped and let out a gasp.

"If a mouse is going to scare you, you better turn back, scaredy cat," she murmured.

She quickly moved down the hall and approached a fork in the path. "Eenie, meenie, miney, mo," she said, remembering the rhyme she and her friends used to say when determining who would be it when they played tag. The luck of the draw had her going down the left path.

She held the broom in front of her with both hands. "I'm okay. It's okay. I can do this."

Something clanged behind her. Jenna twirled around, ready to whack whatever was there. But the corridor was empty. When she started walking again, the metal clunking noise repeated itself. It sounded like chains being dragged across the ground.

She took off running and whatever was making the noise picked up its pace, too. The metal against metal sound reminded her of nails running down a chalkboard. No matter which way she turned, the sound kept following her. But whoever it was stayed out of eyesight. An opening came up on her right, and she ducked inside. The room was dark, except for a triangle of light at the entrance. She pressed her back up against the wall next to the door and waited.

"Little mouse, little mouse," a voice called out. "The cat wants to play."

"Go play with your own catnip," she replied under her breath, her heart pounding as he closed in.

The masked man chuckled. He doubted she was even aware that she'd gone in a circle and was almost back where she started. Not that it mattered, though. She was going to spend the next day or two in the room she'd ducked into, anyway. He was going to make sure of it.

It was time for two days of darkness. She'd have two days of not being able to see anything, including him. But he'd be able to see everything with his infrared cameras and goggles. The fear in her eyes. Her succulent, naked body. Everything.

Jiggling the chains, he whipped them against the dirt wall. Soon, they would be used to tie Jenna to the wall. His jeans grew tight thinking about it. Shoving his hand in his pocket, he adjusted himself as to not cut off his blood supply.

"You may want to run, darling."

Not that the warning would get her moving, but he may as well give her a chance to run. The chase always made things much more fun. He hated it when they cowered in the corner like a timid little animal.

It must be that primal instinct inside every man. The desire to hunt and capture their prey, or when it came to women, club them over the head and drag them back to their cave.

"Jenna," he said, taunting her. "I'm going to lick every inch of your body."

She tightened her grip on the broom handle and murmured, "Over my dead body."

There was no way she was going to go down without a fight. She was no karate master, but what was that saying again, 'Hell hath no fury like a woman scorned?' Okay, maybe she hadn't been scorned, but she was one pissed off woman.

The dirt crunched on the other side of the wall and then everything went quiet. He stopped moving, and she held her breath, waiting for his next move. She had a sneaky suspicion he knew she was there.

"I know you have the broom handle."

Her eyes bugged out, and her jaw dropped. Now she knew for certain there were cameras in the cabin. He was one sick prick. She hoped he would get his goodies in the end and wind up in jail...if she didn't murder him first.

CHAPTER SEVENTEEN

Jenna's body shook as she waited for him to make his move, hoping he would pass her by. Fat chance, though. He knew she was there. It seemed like he always knew what she was doing and where she was going.

She ran her finger over the lump between her index finger and thumb, and a sudden realization dawned on her. He must have injected her with a tracking chip. She'd heard about them, but she knew only top government officials used them or people who worked in the military.

Christian groups were all over the technology, talking about it being the mark of the beast and stuff. She didn't know much about it, but she sure as heck hoped it wasn't the mark. She was already going through hell and didn't really want a double dose of it.

Holding the broom, her knuckles white, she cursed under her breath. The ball in her chest grew with each passing moment. "Go away," she cried.

In a flash, he was in the room, jabbing something into her upper arm. She swung the broom, connecting the end with his stomach. He groaned and fell backwards, hitting his head on the corner of the door frame.

Jenna rushed out of the room and down the hallway. But when she was about twenty feet away, her eyes blurred, and the walls around her spun like a tilt-a-whirl. Off-balance, she leaned against the wall, breathing hard.

"What's happening to me?"

Her legs dropped out from under her, and she slid down the wall, dizzy and lightheaded. When he emerged from the room, she wanted to run, but her body refused to listen. Dragging herself along the ground, her body grew increasingly heavy, until even her arms wouldn't move. He laughed. His chuckle made her stomach twist into a hundred knots.

"Please let me go," she tried to say, but her mouth wouldn't open to form the words.

Grabbing her under the arms, he pulled her into the room. Her spinning vision made the bile from her stomach rise in her throat. Unable to turn her head or lean forward, puke shot out of her mouth, hitting her belly and jacket. The masked man yanked her towards the back wall of the room.

He removed her jacket and then chained her hands to the wall. Her body shook violently as it lay against the cool brown earth. Dirty and dazed, she said, "Please don't." Her words came out garbled and unrecognizable because neither her tongue nor her mouth wanted to move. She wanted to kick him, but she was only an entity in a body that no longer listened to her.

He licked his lips and knelt before her. She could see the hunger in his green eyes and knew exactly what he was thinking, what he wanted. Reaching out, he cupped her breast, playing with them until her nipples pointed to attention. Despite her body being sedated, her nerves were apparently wide awake. *Please, no. Don't touch me!*

Tears filled her eyes as he continued his assault against her breasts. Leaning forward, he licked her nipples, swirling his tongue around and around as he moaned with pleasure.

Stop, please!

She struggled to move, but her body felt like a fish out of water, and she couldn't do anything more than flop around. He slid her body down the wall so that she was laying down, and then he strad-dled her.

"I've been waiting a long time for this," he said. His voice sounded modulated, like he was using some type of device to disguise it.

"Why me?" she cried silently. What had she ever done to deserve this? She just wanted to live her life on her own terms and go where she wanted to go. Was that so wrong? Her body was hers alone to make choices with. That's how it was supposed to be. No one was supposed to take that away from her. Her body, her choice. Right?

The sound of his zipper coming down made her spirit cower in fear and disappear into the corner of her mind, where she couldn't see or feel anything. Tears flowed down her cheeks as her legs were shoved apart.

Think about flowers, a field full of tulips. She was running through the field without a care in the world. The sun was high in the sky. The air rich with the sweet smell of pollen. Deers were munching away on the grass near the tree line. Baby rabbits were jumping around, chasing each other in gleeful play.

She stopped in the middle and spun in circles, arms spread out. Taking in a deep breath, she let it out slowly and then repeated the action. A sharp jab of pain broke her out of her mindfulness dream as her body slowly started to feel again. He was on top of her, inside her.

"No," she tried to cry. In and out he moved, her body crying out in pain from the unwelcome intrusion, her muscles tensing.

"Keep tensing," he moaned deeply, "just like that. It feels so good."

"Ge' off me, ple'," she begged, her words slurring from the drugs.

He just kept moving harder and faster until his own body tensed and jerked against hers. A loud moan ripped from his mouth, and he shuddered. After a few minutes of lying motionless, apparently satis-fied, he kissed her forehead and moved off her.

"Thanks, sweet cheeks, I needed that."

"Go to hell," she muttered as her tongue finally loosened.

"Is that any way to speak to your first lover?"

Gathering all the spit she could, she fired it his way. "I'm going to kill you, I swear."

Wiping the spittle off the front of his shirt, he tucked himself back in his pants and patted her leg. "I'll be back."

He shut the door behind him as he left the room, leaving her in total darkness and alone. The ambience of the room reflected the tortured spirit within her. She hauled herself up to a sitting position. Her body was stiff and sore. Her cries filled the empty room, her shoulders shaking under the heavy weight of her tears.

She lifted her head and cried, "God, how could you let that happen to me?"

Silence.

"What did I do to deserve this?"

Kicking her legs, she banged her heels into the ground. "Why won't you answer me?"

Wasn't he going to help her get out of this mess? She'd done her best to live a moral life and keep herself pure for her future husband. Her parents drilled that lesson into her from a young age, but now...

She was glad to be in the dark, and she didn't have to look at her dirty, ugly ass body sitting there on the ground. *Damn it. Damn it.* She was so stupid. No wonder she was in this mess. If she'd only stayed inside the club, she'd be safe and sound. Maybe she deserved everything she had coming. Defeated, she leaned her head back against the wall and let the tears fall, her uncertain future dangling before her eyes.

Would he be back? Jenna shivered, her body brushing abrasively against the dirt. Cringing in pain, she attempted to do her breathing techniques to calm her nerves. When she tried to breathe out, a loud sob burst forth as she recalled the feel of him inside her.

Screaming, she kicked her heels into the ground. *Let this be a bad dream. Please, don't let this be real.* The ache between her thighs told her the truth of the matter, though. Her stomach churned and whatever remained in her stomach slid up her throat, spilling onto the ground beside her. Heave after heave rocked her body until there was nothing left.

Her skin crawled, still sensing the touch of his fingers, like thousands of tiny spiders making her body their home. "Go away!" she cried.

Please, go away.

She rubbed her legs together to stop an itch and tensed when she felt her damp crotch. Fresh tears burned her eyes. No one was going to want to touch her now. No guy was ever going to give her a second look. She was garbage. Trash. The only ones who were going to want her were men like her abductor or dumpster divers who didn't care where their garbage had been.

"Why me?" she cried.

All she wanted to do was crawl into a grave and die. She wouldn't even be able to look her mother or father in the eyes ever again after this. They would look at her with such contempt and wish she'd never been born.

Nobody loved damaged goods. They always sent them back to the factory. And that's all she was. She couldn't even get a redo on life. No one could ever put her body back together again.

There would be no wonderful first for her. No guy to whisper sweet words of love into her ear as he took her virginity. Something that she believed belonged to her true love. She squeezed her eyes closed, trying to erase the masked man's image from her mind and how her nipples responded to him. *Oh god, I'm a whore.*

"Damn you," she cried into the darkness.

CHAPTER EIGHTEEN

Detective Charleston knew his hunches were correct and the report in his hands confirmed it. Craig's birth certificate was indeed a fake. That didn't surprise him in the slightest. Even the people he mentioned as his parents were a figment of his imagination. There were no records of them anywhere.

Since Johnathan found out about him, he had his team hanging around the guy's house doing surveillance. He never came back though, or if he did, no one saw him. The man was like a ghost. It took them a while, but they finally got a warrant to search his place. They were heading over there this morning to turn it upside down.

It's been over a week since Jenna disappeared and Christmas was less than a week away. He couldn't even begin to imagine what a bitter holiday it would be for the McCays if he couldn't find some way to bring her home.

Just thinking about not having his own little girl with him, seeing her smiling and giggling as she opened her presents, tore at his heart. His world would be such a dark place if his baby disappeared. That was why he knew he couldn't leave any stone unturned.

As John stared blankly at the report, Clyde poked his head in the door, saying, "Ready to go when you are."

"Give me a minute, and I'll meet you outside."

John picked up his coffee and downed the last few remaining drops that had been sitting there, cold and stale. Coughing, his face twisted in disgust. He probably looked like he just swallowed a lemon.

Hopefully, they would find something at Craig's place and be able to give Jenna's family some good news for a change, instead of the same damn information. It was killing him to have to tell them that they hadn't found her yet. Her mother called at the same time every day. The lady was like bloody clockwork, and he was beginning to sound like a broken record.

He straightened the pile of papers on his desk, organizing them in to-do piles for later, and then shut down his computer. John turned his head and then groaned. His trapeze muscle had seized, preventing him from turning his head to the left. Oh, the joys of getting old.

Satisfied that his desk was left in the condition he wanted it, he grabbed his jacket off the back of the chair, his hat off the hook, and then joined Clyde outside.

His partner grinned when he saw him. "When are you going to catch up with the times? You look like Sherlock Holmes."

"Comfort over modern, my dear fellow."

Clyde roared with laughter. "Oh god! You even have his voice down pat. I bet you use a magnifying glass when you go down on your wife."

John punched him in the shoulder before sitting in the driver's seat. "Jerk."

His partner walked around to the other side of the car and climbed in. "Asshole."

"Fart face."

"Tinkerbell."

Putting the car in reverse, John pulled out of the parking spot. "Seriously, Tinkerbell?"

Grinning, Clyde shrugged his shoulders. "I swear the kids have made me watch Peter Pan like a million times recently. I'm liable to start flying."

"Better than Barney. My daughter has that dinosaur attached to her hip. She makes me sing the Barney song when I put her to bed."

"I love you. You love me—"

"Shut up before I bruise your other shoulder," John said. He tried to sound annoyed but the grin on his face betrayed him.

They lapsed into silence. The situation before them was grim, and they knew it. A bit of joking around didn't change the circumstances any. Chances were high that they would recover a body and not a warm, live person, but he wasn't about to lose hope. It was what kept him going.

"Don't worry, John. We'll find her."

All he could do was nod, keeping his eyes trained on the road. The atmosphere in the car changed from light-hearted to dark and dreary. He knew they could be walking into another dead end, but John kept his fingers crossed.

Pulling up to the house, he saw the door wide open and the other half of his team already inside working. He hoped they weren't barking up the wrong tree, and Phillip was right about this. If Craig wasn't their guy, they were wasting valuable time that Jenna didn't have.

John turned the engine off and placed his hand on the handle. "Let's do this thang."

Hours later, they finally had a locksmith on site to get into a safe that had been discovered behind a picture of a human skeleton in living room. On the desk in the corner sat a heart in a glass container, filled with what smelled like formaldehyde.

A tall V bookcase was positioned in the corner of the room and the shelves were filled with bones and skulls. Johnathan had a feeling they weren't dealing with a mere janitor here. The guy had a human anatomy fetish.

"Do you think they are all human bones?" John asked Wynn, one of his leading forensic technicians.

"Wouldn't surprise me."

"Bag 'em and tag 'em, will ya?"

"I was just heading out to the car to get my equipment."

John gave him a pat on the shoulder when he walked by. The twenty-nine-year-old fit in well with his team and was always one step ahead of him. Once he got the bones back to the lab, they might be able to find out who, or what, they belonged to. Upon hearing a click, he turned to find that the locksmith had managed to get the square wall safe open.

"Thanks, Jeff." John stuck out his hand.

Taking his hand, the locksmith said, "No problem. Call me anytime." As he was about to head out of the room, the man turned around. "Any news on the girl yet?"

"I'm hoping the news might be in the safe you just cracked."

"Good luck."

"Thanks, man. We're gonna need it."

He bid the guy good-bye and then reached into the safe.

Again and again, the masked man came into the damp, dark room. He would seize her, force her to open to him until her entire body was numb. Dead of all feelings. Each time, she lost a little more of herself. A little more of who she used to be, becoming only a dessert for a crazed man's appetite.

Unable to cry any longer, unable to scream, Jenna lay there covered in dirt. Her voice hoarse. Her throat dry. He'd given her next to no food or water. All he did was take, take and take, even when she had nothing left to give.

The room felt like her crypt. A place she was doomed to spend eternity. Where her skin would rot, and her eyes would be eaten by worms. Was this hell? She couldn't imagine a worse place to be than this.

"God, let me die!" she cried, her throat burning with each word. Almost as much as her backside as she lay in her own filth. Was this what God had in store for her? Was this payback for not following him completely?

"What do you want from me?"

Just then, the door opened, and the room flooded with a pale light. She recognized his shadow in the door as her eyes adjusted to the invasion. Jenna tried to hide herself in the darkness, cowering in the corner. Please, not again. Not so soon.

The man stood there in the door, unmoving. She closed her eyes and made herself as small as possible, wishing for him to go away. But she knew he wouldn't. He wouldn't leave until he got what he came for.

Her throbbing vagina recoiled at his presence, tensing painfully. "Not again. Please." There was no way her body could handle another round of his abuse. His shoes crunched the dirt beneath his feet as he walked towards her. The sound made her heart race and her stomach roll. Stopping in front of her, he knelt down.

"Please don't," she whimpered, her own voice unrecognizable to her.

Feeling something pressing against her lips, she turned her head to the side. He gripped the top of her head and turned it back towards him.

"Go away!" she cried.

"Drink." He shoved something towards her, clanking it against her teeth. She cautiously opened one eye and saw a glass full of liquid.

Turning her head away again, she closed her mouth, locking her teeth together. Again, with a firm grip on her head, he tilted it back and poured the water against her lips. The moment the water hit her lips, a well of thirst burst open inside her, and she hungrily lapped up every drop he gave her.

"Good girl," he said, patting her leg.

Both his eyes and his voice were familiar, but they didn't seem to go together. Was her mind even working properly anymore? The harder she concentrated, the blurrier things became, until she could no longer make out the man in front of her anymore.

A warmth flooded her body, and she found herself struggling to keep her eyes open. "No!" She didn't want to sleep, couldn't sleep while he was here. But she couldn't stop it. Her chin dropped to her chest, and she was pulled from one world into another.

CHAPTER NINETEEN

Hot air circled around Jenna. While breathing in, the air was so stifling that it felt like a blanket was covering her face. Opening her eyes, she found herself staring into a sheet of blurry glass or plastic about a foot away from her face.

Trapped.

Stretching her arms out, her elbows rammed into the solid surface, shaking the ground beneath her. The movement resulted in something brushing against her right cheek. Turning her head, she found herself eye to eye with a spider the size of her hand.

She froze, afraid to move as it moved its fangs up and down. Swallowing hard, she bit back a cry of panic, not wanting to kiss those ugly, hairy fangs. Her heart was running as wild as her imagination. They could suck her dry like a vampire if they wanted to.

But there would be no Stephen, or Edward, from the make-believe world of vampires to rescue her. She was in this alone. Invisible hands wrapped around her airway, constricting her ability to breathe. With short, shallow breaths, she reached up with her left hand to push the sheet of plastic away.

It wouldn't move.

A tickle moved across her bare leg. Lifting her head slightly, she could see more movement. Oh Shit. Shit. Shit. There was more than one spider. Oh God. She was dead or was going to be soon.

Her chin wobbled and fear spun inside her body like a web, making her shake from her head to her toes. Out of the corner of her eye, she saw the spider flick something into the air. Sharp needle-point hairs embedded into her cheek. Squeezing her eyes closed, she stifled another cry as her cheek burned with red-hot pain, itching like mad, but she didn't dare scratch.

The spider on her leg slowly crawled up her body. She had to fight to stay still and not try to shake it off. Every pore of her being cried out for her to react. Even her spirit was going whacko.

She bit back a scream and fought against another full body tremor. Was this what it felt like when a ghost walked over your grave? She didn't like it. Not even in the slightest. The movement resulted in more hairs being fired her way. Some landed on her cheek, others on her abdomen. Her stomach contracted at the contact, and she cringed, tears pooling in her eyes.

Jenna tried to find solace in the fact that they hadn't dug their thick, juicy fangs into her yet, but that did little to quell her fears. She had no way out, and no idea when the pervert would free her from the glass-like coffin.

Closing her eyes, she tried to forget where she was, even with the spider approaching her breasts. But all her mind could focus on was each individual touch of its legs as it moved across her stomach, sending micro shivers through her body.

When the front leg of the spider touched her chin, her body jerked, sending the spider's fangs deep into her skin. She picked it up and threw it to the end of the coffin, where it dug its fangs into her foot.

"God, let me out of here," Jenna screamed. Unable to contain herself any longer, she banged against the lid. The force of her pounding knocked the legs out from under her coffin, bringing it and her crashing to the ground.

The lid popped off, and she sprung out of her prison, sending the spiders scurrying into the corner. She rushed towards the door, and to her surprise, it wasn't locked. She stood there for a moment in shock.

Upon hearing a noise down the hall, she took off in the opposite direction, attempting to wipe the spider hairs off her cheek and getting some stuck in her hand in the process. Shaking, Jenna mumbled, "I hate spiders."

Finding a ladder, she climbed it, butt naked. She had no idea where her jacket was anymore. Halfway up to the hatch, cool air nipped at her bare skin, covering her in so many goosebumps that she probably looked like a chicken.

Jenna pushed at the hatch, but it barely moved. Giving it a harder shove, it opened further, and white cool powder landed on her head. Snow! This must lead to a spot outside the cabin. With a new burst of energy, she pushed at the lid with all the strength she could muster, and it flipped open.

The full brunt of the cool air made her gasp as it moved like a cyclone around her, tempting her to retreat back into the tunnel. But the crunching of shoes on the dirt below gave her the gumption she needed to climb outside.

If she didn't get help, was she going to die from the spider bite? What kind of spider was it? Was it a tarantula? Weren't they venomous? Oh god. She didn't know a thing about spiders, and now she was wishing she would have studied them more.

Standing up, Jenna found herself in a field that looked awfully familiar. Turning in a circle, she found herself face to face with the door to the cabin. The jerk must have numerous trap doors situated around the place.

Hearing a noise from below, she glanced down the hole and found the masked man on his way up the ladder, holding a knife in his hand. She slammed the hatch closed and stood on top. Her body was shivering endlessly from the cold, and her feet stung from being covered in snow.

The man attempted to open the hatch numerous times before the banging stopped. She wasn't sure if he was gone or just playing another game, but she was too cold to find out. He had apparently removed the lock from the door to the cabin. She opened the door and ducked inside out of the weather.

Not that the cabin was much warmer. The fireplace was as dead as her feet were going to be if she didn't get a fire going soon. She pushed the couch in front of the door before moving to the corner of the cabin to grab some logs to light a fire.

She wished she could have kept running, but not having any clothes meant that she had no chance in hell of surviving the brutal weather. Once she got the fire going, she walked over to the bed to grab the sheets and gasped in shock.

Her clothes were sitting on the pillow, clean and folded. Narrowing her eyes, she wondered whether he'd placed talcum powder in them or something. She grabbed her shirt and turned it inside out, checking every inch of the material. Satisfied that it was clean enough, she slipped it over her head and revelled in the feel of the material against her skin.

She stared at her underwear as a creepy feeling flowed through her. Picking them up, she tossed them into the fire and just slipped on her black pants. The man even left her shoes and jacket over by the table.

Why had he given her the clothes back? Was he trying to set her up to run again, only to trap her some other way? She couldn't understand why he didn't barge into the cabin when he was right behind her and take her back to the dungeon.

Her head was spinning with questions and there were no answers she could think of. Still cold, she grabbed the comforter and laid it on the floor in front of the fire. Covering herself with the sheets, she snuggled as close to the fire as she could.

All the while, praying for a way out of the mess she found herself in.

"Are you serious?" John asked in disbelief. He thought he'd finally stumbled onto something, and it, too, fell through the floor.

"Unfortunately. His mother died when he was nineteen, and his father passed away last year. I mean, we could try talking to his grandparents and see if they know anything, but it doesn't sound like he's been to see them in years," his partner, Clyde, said as he munched on an apple.

Johnathan growled. He hated dead ends. Picking up his coffee mug, he tossed it across the room, shattering it into tiny pieces when it hit the wall. Coffee dripped down the wallpaper, pooling at the base.

"Do we have a list of properties that their family owns? Jenna has to be somewhere," John said.

"I'll check into it. Here's the info on the grandparents, David and Judith Graham, if you want to chat with them. Oh, I forgot to mention, his real name is Mathew Graham, not Craig. Good ole Lisa tracked down his real birth certificate based on the DNA sample you gave me from his hairbrush."

Holding out his hand, John accepted the paper from Clyde. He supposed there was no harm in going and speaking with the grandparents. Looking at the information, he noted that they were in their late 80s and were residents at an assisted living complex in Toronto.

Clyde turned and walked towards the door, pausing before going through. "You might want to call social services as well. It looks like his family had some dealings with them years ago, prior to when Craig went into the psych ward."

John raised an eyebrow at his partner. "Do you know why he was admitted?"

Clyde shook his head. "I haven't had a chance to look into it yet."

Well, that gave him a few more things to work with to keep his mind occupied. It was the day before Christmas Eve, and, in the spirit of the season, he couldn't let his mind be beaten by the darkness that his job often carried with it.

He called the office of the assisted living complex and inquired about the health of Craig's—correction—Mathew's parents. His grandmother was lucid, but unfortunately, his grandfather was touched by dementia and wasn't easy to carry on a conversation with.

His call was transferred to their room. "Hello?" a raspy feminine voice answered, followed by a coughing fit.

"Hi, Mrs. Graham, I'm Detective Charleston with the Surrey RCMP. I'm calling in regards to your grandson."

"Which one?"

Surprised, he found himself at a loss for words, his mouth opening and closing in silence. He was under the impression they only had one.

"Hello? Are you still there, Detective?" she asked.

CHAPTER TWENTY

Gasping, Jenna woke up, forehead dripping with sweat. "Get off me," she screamed, kicking and clawing at the empty air. She jumped up and promptly fell over, her feet tangling in the sheets. Groaning, she rolled over and stared at the ceiling. Where was she? She wasn't in the cell or anywhere in the tunnels. Small particles of dust hovered in the air, glowing in the morning light, and birds chirped outside the window beside her.

Was it all a dream? It had to be. She was still in the cabin and wearing her clothes, but as soon as she stood up, she knew she was lying to herself. Her pants brushed against her inner thighs, and she cringed. Slowly, she slipped her pants down and saw that her skin was rubbed raw, bleeding.

Collapsing to the floor, she burst into tears, hugging her legs close to her chest. "Why me?" She could still feel him inside her, could still smell the garlic and onion caked on his lips. Jenna spat on the floor, rubbing her lips viciously.

Tears blurred her vision, but that was fine by her. She didn't want to see her body, to see his marks that marred her innocent skin. Or not so innocent skin. A knot welled up inside her. Standing up, she moved towards the kitchen. Her agony so great it threatened to break her open like a nutcracker.

How could he have done that to her? She picked up a kitchen chair and threw it across the room, screaming as loud as she could. Grabbing the edge of the table, she flipped it and kicked it into the corner.

Little by little, she tore the place apart, pulling everything off the wall and shelves. "I'm going to kill you, you asshole." Lifting the clock off its hanger, she threw it against the wall, dislodging a small black box from its base.

Picking up the box, she turned it over and over in her hands. "What the heck?" In the centre of the box, there appeared to be a tiny lens, no bigger than the head of a pen. It looked like a camera.

She may not be this super tech, wizard type person, but she knew a camera when she saw one. Placing it on the floor, she smacked it with the clock, breaking both into smaller pieces. She kept on hitting it until there was nothing left to break, tears streaming down her face.

Wasn't anyone going to come for her? Why couldn't they find her? Couldn't they track her through her phone's GPS or something? It was like everyone had abandoned her to this crazy fool. Discarded her like she was no better than trash in a garbage can.

Didn't anyone love her anymore? Didn't she matter? She massaged her chest, trying to ease the ache that had become as permanent as the frown etched into her face. She didn't want to continue this game, didn't want to face another moment with him.

After putting on her shoes, she moved the couch away from the door and opened it, breathing in deeply. The fresh air renewed her strength and helped her find the courage to make her next move.

She made her way back to the pit with the wolf, listening carefully to all the sounds around her. Looking over the side, she covered her nose as the smell of the decaying wolf permeated the air. The pit was too wide to jump across. The only thing she could do was climb down and attempt to climb up the other side, but that didn't look too promising. No footholds.

Glancing at the bushes alongside the pit, she wondered if she could hold on to them and shimmy her way across. She didn't relish the idea of the thin branches snapping though and sending her backwards into the pit again. The thought of seeing the remains of the wolf a third time made her want to puke.

Getting a decent hold on the bush, she started to work her way along the left side, testing each section before letting go of the last. Hope rose within her as she neared the opposite side. There was a light at the end of her long, dark tunnel, and it grew brighter with each step.

When she reached the other side, Jenna took off running. Away from the cabin. Away from the pit. Away from him. Her raw thighs stung as she ran through the forest. She wasn't sure how long she had been running for when the sound of running water almost burst her ear drums. Rushing towards the sound, she skidded to a halt, her feet inches away from going over a cliff.

She looked over the edge and whistled. "Damn." The waters below smashed tirelessly against the jutting rocks, white caps skimming across the surface. With her head spinning, she slowly backed away and sat down on a rock. Her body heavy with disappointment.

There was nowhere for her to go. No way for her to get away. She'd tried every other direction. This was her last hope. What was left for her? There was no way she was going to return to the cabin and continue to be his plaything. She'd rather die. With great consternation, Jenna realized there was no other option if she wanted peace.

In that moment, she felt like she stepped outside herself as she watched her body move towards the edge of the cliff. Fighting the internal battle of what must be done, and yet, crying out for a life she still had yet to live.

Tears streamed down her cheeks, flooding her lips with their sweet, salty taste. Her dreams were never meant to be. Her dad would never know the exhilaration of walking her down the aisle, giving her away. Her womb would never know the joy of holding a life within its walls. She'd never know what it was like to hold a newborn baby in her arms.

Hiccupping, Jenna stared at the rushing waters below. Would it hurt when her body hit the rocks? Was there an afterlife? Would God understand if she took her own life? She certainly hoped so, because that was all she had now. She wished she could say good-bye to her family one last time. To hold her mom and dad close and let them know how much she loved them. Ask for forgiveness for all the times she rebelled and fought with them over the years.

For all the times, she got mad at her mom for holding her back because of her anxiety, refusing to let her go out. She could still remember every missed opportunity, and why the kids in her class finally stopped asking her to go anywhere, pulling away from her, calling her a momma's girl.

"But, Mom, all the other kids are allowed to go. Why can't I?" she would beg.

"If all the other kids jumped off a bridge, would you do it?"

"It's not fair!"

"I said no and that's final."

She'd looked at her dad with pleading eyes, but he was no help. He'd learned quickly that there was no convincing her mom of anything, so he'd just disappear into his study. Eventually, she gave up trying and allowed herself to be the wallflower of the class. There, but not there, according to her classmates.

Ironic, wasn't it? The question from her mom about the bridge, and now, here she stood on the precipice of making that very choice. It was Christmas Eve, and the greatest gift she could give herself was to step off this cliff. How sad was that?

Would anyone find her body? Would her parents have to come and identify her? The idea bubbled like acid in her stomach. She didn't want them to have to see her all mangled and torn, but it was her only answer to freedom. To finally fly high and be the angel hovering over them.

Maybe God, if he existed, would let her be her mom's guardian angel and finally be able to help her be at peace instead of afraid all the time. She didn't want her mom to feel pain anymore, just wanted her to live a happy life for once.

Pulling out her phone, she left her mom a quick message about what was happening and why she made the choice to jump. She wasn't sure if her mom would ever get the message, but hopefully she'd understand and find peace with her decision. She knew her mom wouldn't want her to keep suffering at the hands of a mad man. But would she blame herself? Would her mom blame her dad for not being around?

"Please, forgive me, Mom." Jenna took a moment to look up into the big blue expanse above her. "God, whoever and wherever you are, take care of them for me."

Toeing the edge of the cliff, she spread her arms wide. She closed her eyes and leaned forward. As she went over the cliff, a noise from behind startled her.

"Jenna, No!"

Turning as she fell, she caught a glimpse of a figure running towards her.

CHAPTER TWENTY-ONE

With Jenna's shirt bunched in his fist, Derek yelled, "Grab my hand!"

Her eyes widened, her body quaking in fear as she dangled off the cliff. It initially felt like the right choice. But now, as she stared at the waters below, her feet scrambling to find an anchor, she realized she wasn't ready to die.

Reaching up, she went to take Derek's hand, her mind and heart racing. It's him. Don't let him take you back. She hesitated with fear, frozen in time.

"Damn it, Jenna. Take my hand," he demanded.

Despite her mind's cry, she allowed his hand to wrap around hers. Her sudden desire for survival outranked her desire to have a splatter party on the jagged rocks below. Grunting, he pulled her up to solid ground.

When her feet hit the soil, he attempted to wrap his arms around her, but she shoved him away. "Get away from me," she cried. Breathing hard, she rested her hands on her knees. She was alive.

He rubbed his chest. "Gee, you sure know how to make a guy feel welcome."

"H-how—what...?" she stammered, at a loss for words. "Where'd you come from?"

"What the hell happened that night, Jenna? You were with me and then you were gone. Have you been here this whole time?"

"How-how'd you find me?" She shivered when his familiar green eyes bore into hers. It had to be him. Why else would he be here? No one knew where she was.

Derek pulled his cellphone out of his pocket. "GPS."

Slowly backing away from him, she said, "I haven't had reception since I got here."

He shrugged his shoulders. "All I know is that one day you weren't showing up, and today you did."

"Why didn't you call the police?"

Anger flashed through his eyes, his nostrils flaring. "I didn't know if you had enough time to wait for them to make up their damn minds."

He took a step towards her, but she picked up a stick, brandishing it like a sword. "Stay away from me."

"You think I did this?" he asked, his hands rolling into fists.

Tightening her two-handed grip on the stick, she continued to hold it in front of her as she backed away.

"Jenna, you know me."

She shook her head, tears forming in her eyes. She wanted to believe him, but his eyes belonged to her abuser. He was the same build, and he was here. Not the police. Not her family. Him. "You had my jacket. And it's out here with me. You wanted to make out with me, and h-he, he..." Her throat closed, and she gasped for air, her heart pounding erratically at the memory.

It had to be him. The masked guy was nowhere to be found, and suddenly Derek showed up, brazen, blonde hair and all. He approached her, and she swung the stick at him, connecting it with his shoulder.

Taking advantage of his body being off balance, she took off in the direction of the cabin. Again. Damn it. She didn't want to go back there. Racing through the forest and squeezing around the pit, she reached the clearing and came to an abrupt halt, her feet sliding along the snow. She gasped as she fell over backwards, landing on her butt.

Next to the cabin stood Phillip, the guy from the Janitor's room at the library, his bald head sparkling in the sunlight. The movie 'Twilight' came to mind as she saw the sun's rays falling like diamonds on his head.

Looking back over her shoulder, she spotted Derek closing in on her. "Come on, give me a break," she cried. The two men were getting closer and closer. The moment Derek entered the clearing, Phillip trained his gun on him.

Derek put his hands up in surrender. "Easy there, dude. I'm the good guy."

"Jenna, come here," Phillip said, beckoning her with his free hand. "I'll protect you."

"Don't listen to him, Jenna. How do you think he knew you were here?"

"You're both crazy," she cried, glancing back and forth between the two men, confused as ever. Phillip kept motioning for her to come, keeping his eyes on Derek. Her stomach flip-flopped endlessly as she found herself caught between them with nowhere to go.

"How'd you guys find me?" she asked, narrowing her eyes at them.

"I already told you, you showed up on my GPS." Derek tried to take a step towards her, but Phillip cocked the gun, warding him off. He stopped and glared at the man. "What about you, baldy?"

"Simple. I followed you," Phillip said.

"You aren't going to believe him, are you, Jenna?"

She placed her head in her hands, her body shaking. Her mind was a muddled mess, uncertainty lighting up every corner. Phillip had been following her, but Derek was the last one to have her jacket. A band of pressure wrapped around her head, squeezing it, threatening to pop it like a balloon. "I..." Fear stole the words from her lips. She didn't know who to trust.

"It's okay. The police are on their way," Phillip said calmly.

"Who are you?" she asked him.

"I'm a private investigator."

"How convenient," Derek scoffed. "You'd say anything to get her to go back with you."

Jenna stood up and moved out of the line of fire, the three of them forming a triangle. She wanted to run, but had nowhere to run. The damn collar around her neck cut off every visible exit.

Her eyes widened as an idea flashed through her mind. If she could make it to the cabin and lock the guys outside, she'd be able to get down into the tunnel. But if the kidnapper was Phillip, he'd just shoot Derek and come after her. If it was Derek, then maybe having a gun pointed at him might give her enough time to find her way through the tunnels and stumble upon her freedom.

Step by slow agonizing step, as to not alert them, she moved backwards toward the opposite side of the cabin. The loud cry of a red-tailed hawk caught their attention as it swooped through the clearing, picking up something from the grass. With the men distracted by the bird, she chose that moment to run.

Before she reached the door of the cabin, a deafening gunshot had her sprawling on the ground. She covered her ears, cringing. It was followed by another two shots that echoed through the air, and an ear-piercing human cry.

Getting up, she slowly walked back towards the corner of the cabin. Her body froze instantly, as though someone glued her feet to the snow. There, standing on the edge of the forest, was the masked perpetrator. The other two men were motionless, prostrate on the ground.

She swallowed hard, her throat dry as his eyes connected with hers. A grin slowly spread across his face. He walked over to Phillip and picked up his gun, giving him another kick. Turning, Jenna raced into the cabin and shut the door, pushing the couch in front of the door.

Opening the trapdoor, she climbed down the ladder and raced down the long corridor to the fork in the tunnel. Knowing he wouldn't be too far behind, she took the direction she hadn't gone before. She moved as fast as her sore and tired legs would go.

An open door caught her attention, and she stopped to look inside. Computer monitors were everywhere, each showing a different picture of the cabin and the yard. One monitor was blank. It had nothing more than grey fuzzy lines. That must have been the camera she found in the clock.

Upon hearing a noise down the passageway, she frantically looked around the room for an exit. In a darkened corner, she saw an almost invisible door blending in with the dirt walls. Dodging in and out of the equipment scattered throughout the room, she made her way over to it and threw it open.

Behind it were wooden spiral stairs leading up to what she presumed to be the surface.

"Hey, stop," his voice called from the other side of the room. Her heart did a triple beat, sending a shooting pain into her shoulder and down her arm. Anxiety ricocheted through her.

Please don't let me have a heart attack now.

Holding her hand to her chest, she spun around and took the stairs two at a time. "Please open. Please open!" Jenna begged as she neared the trapdoor. If it didn't budge, she was trapped.

Reaching the top step, she pushed on the wooden trapdoor. "Shit. Shit." It wouldn't budge. Not again! She could hear him getting closer and closer. Banging on the door, she cried out, "Someone help me!"

Jenna struggled to breathe, her airway closing in on her. She couldn't do this, couldn't let him take her again. Feeling much like a trapped animal, she paced the small step as the man she came to dread stopped below her.

He reached up to grab her ankle, and she kicked out at him. "Leave me alone," she cried, banging again on the trapdoor. "Someone please help me."

In that moment, the trapdoor squeaked open above her.

CHAPTER TWENTY-TWO

"Damn it! Can't you drive any faster?" John growled, hitting the dash with his fist.

"Maybe buy a race car next time instead of this Volkswagen. It's slower than hell."

"Hey, don't be hatin' on the car. It was a good deal."

"Me be hatin'? You just punched the damn thing," Clyde said with a cheeky grin.

John's knuckles itched to connect with his buddy's shoulder, but he considered against it since the man was driving. He didn't exactly want to find himself wrapped around a tree. It may be Christmas, but he wasn't a decoration.

His friend was right, though. His car wasn't exactly a vehicle that would come out on top in a race or a chase. But it was inconspicuous and didn't stand out, which worked great for the undercover work they usually did. Mind you, they had the lights on the dash now as they snail-raced down the back roads.

"Just drive, Grandma."

Just then, his partner took a sharp corner, barely slowing down. John grabbed onto the armrest.

"Like that?" Clyde asked.

John rolled his eyes. "Remind me to bop you one when my stomach settles."

He wasn't sure if the butterflies in his stomach were a result of the roller coaster type road they were driving down or if it was because they were about to solve the case. This was the closest he'd come to nailing the perpetrator. And it would be the first live rescue if they got there in time.

Glancing at his watch, a dark cloud of worry descended upon him. Phillip missed his check-in call. Granted, he probably just forgot, which fit his character perfectly, but it didn't sit well with John. Without his update, they could be walking into a trap and not know it.

Dialling Phillip's number again, he waited for a response, but it went to voicemail. John slapped the cellphone on his lap. Nothing made him more irritated than a blind spot. Looking in the side mirror, he sighed in relief as the vehicles carrying their back-up appeared behind them. Six other team members were along for the ride besides the two of them.

In the distance, he saw a dark, cloudy tendril drifting into the sky, presumably from a fireplace. "We're getting close. Everyone, stay alert," he said over the radio.

"10-4," a voice on the radio replied.

The rest of the team responded with their personal call signs and confirmed that they understood. Each person had their own instructions of what to do and where to go. They were going to approach the cabin from all four angles, cutting off any escape route, if possible.

The cabin was about a ten to fifteen minute hike from the main road, so they were going to have to go in on foot. He didn't really know this area of the woods, but Clyde had been here before.

A friend from Search and Rescue had also confirmed the location of the cabin when he flew over the area about an hour ago. Thankfully, there didn't appear to be anyone visibly guarding the place according to the aerial view, which was good, but he was still uneasy.

When Clyde pulled the car to a stop. The men behind them

followed suit. Getting out of the vehicle, they all gathered around the trunk of the car to check the map one last time.

"Does everyone understand?" John asked.

"Hey boss, look at this," one of his men said, pulling the branches off a hidden green car tucked away in a small clearing across the road.

"Tom and Kevin, stay with the vehicle and see what you can find. Radio us if you see anyone."

"Aw, can't anyone else babysit the car?" Kevin complained.

John knew they wanted a piece of the action and couldn't blame them, but someone needed to stay behind. "You have your orders."

He turned towards the others. "Any questions?"

His men shook their heads. Pulling his gun out of the holster, he led the way into the forest. Eager to get this over and done with. His dream of bringing her home for Christmas was hopefully about to come true, but he couldn't let himself get cocky. Bad things happen when you get overconfident.

Seeing the cabin through the trees, John put a finger to his lips, motioning the men to be quiet. Using hand signals, he directed them to where he wanted them to go. He and Clyde were going to enter first, and the others were to stay hidden.

On the far side of the clearing, he saw a body on the ground. He approached it, with Clyde flanking his side. Kneeling down, he rolled the body over. It was Phillip, his eyes wide open, giving him a blank stare. Blood covered the front of his holey shirt. John's heart sank, and he cursed under his breath.

Looking up at his current partner, Johnathan shook his head. "Damn it all to hell! Why didn't he wait for us?"

Clyde let a hand rest on his partner's shoulder for a moment as a lone tear slipped down John's cheek.

John stood up, his wet eyes cold and hard. "Let's find that asshole."

~

When the trapdoor fully opened, she looked up. Derek stood above her, clutching his shoulder, fury written all over his face. Instead of helping her out to the surface, he forced his way down, pushing her towards the other guy.

"What are you doing?" she cried.

Hauling her back into the room, he shoved her into a chair before turning to glare at the masked man. "Damn it, Craig. You weren't supposed to shoot me."

The masked man reached behind his head and pulled off the mask, revealing a head full of dark brown hair. "Gee thanks, bro."

Jenna gasped, "You!"

"And me," Derek said, waving at her. His fake facade was completely gone.

"I-I don't understand."

She'd worked with both of them ever since she started at the library. Craig, the janitor, had always been friendly, even offered to take her out for a night on the town, as he called it. She'd refused, of course, but he didn't seem to take it too hard, or at least she thought he hadn't.

"Of course, you wouldn't, little miss innocent. Oh wait, not so innocent now, are you?" Derek said, running his fingers along her shoulder. "You were wonderful."

Jenna cringed, choking back a sob as fresh memories broke to the surface. Every sensation from that moment was as alive now as it was then. "How could you?" she cried.

"All part of the game," Craig said, tossing Derek a towel. "Stop dripping blood on my floor."

"It's your fault. You're the one who shot me."

"So sue me."

"Why can't you ever stick to the plan? I was supposed to rescue her and be the hero."

"I wasn't done with her yet."

"Hell, man, she tried to kill herself. You told me you wouldn't let it go that far."

"Aw, did my foster bro go and fall in love with the test subject?"

"Screw you," Derek said, shoving him. "You knew I liked her. That's why we planned this whole thing, remember?"

"That's what I let you think."

With the room spinning, Jenna placed her head between her legs, trying to process everything that was happening. Derek was here. Craig was here. It couldn't be them. She had to be hallucinating. She knew them...spent time with them.

"This can't be happening," she whispered. Upon hearing a crunch and a howl, she looked up to see Craig's nose bent and blood dripping down his face, his eyes blazing. He pulled the gun out of the back of his pants and pointed it at Derek, who quickly grabbed his hand. A shot rang out. Screaming, Jenna dove to the ground as the bullet embedded itself into the wall behind the chair she'd just been sitting on.

The men wrestled for control of the gun. She crawled across the floor towards the exit, praying they would be too absorbed in their own quarrel to notice. She got to the top of the step before an agonizing burn ripped through her calf, followed by the sound of a gunshot.

Collapsing, Jenna cried out in pain and grabbed onto the railing to stop from falling down the stairs.

"You asshole," Derek yelled, tackling Craig to the ground. "Run, Jenna."

She sat there in a daze, spots floating in front of her eyes. The sharp excruciating pain in her leg overwhelmed her senses as realization dawned on her. She'd been shot.

"Damn it, Jenna. Run!" When she didn't move, Derek pointed the gun her way. "If you don't run, I'll shoot you myself."

He didn't need to tell her twice. One bullet hole was enough. Pulling herself up to the surface, Jenna looked around. She had no idea which way to go. Bushes surrounded her on every side, and she found it hard to concentrate with her leg throbbing.

As she stood there, her eyebrows squished in confusion, another gunshot rang out from below, and then she heard footsteps. Not wanting to find out who was coming up the stairs, she tried to take a step but fell to her knees in agony.

Crawling, she pulled herself behind a large tree and prayed he wouldn't find her, despite the path of blood that followed her. She held her breath, her heart beating rapidly, palms clammy.

"Oh, Jenna," Craig said in a sing-song tone. "It's me!"

CHAPTER TWENTY-THREE

Jenna could feel her life force being drained out of her as her blood soaked the ground beneath her. Staring up at the clear blue sky, she wondered if it would be the last time she'd ever see it. The bucket containing her hopes and dreams was now crushed beyond repair.

He was only a couple of feet away from her. *Oh, god, why me?*

Was this all her life was worth? If this was all that was left for her in this world, why was she even born? An overwhelming throb in her calf had her biting her cheeks to prevent herself from crying out, but she couldn't stop a groan from escaping. She hit her hand on the ground beside her, connecting with a stick. Jenna picked it up just as Craig came around the tree.

Shoving it at him with all her might, the broken end of the stick pierced his stomach. He dropped to his knees, and the gun flew out of his hand. "You bitch."

"Takes one to know one," she quipped, scrambling for the gun.

He jabbed his finger into the wound on her leg and she screamed in pain as she kicked at him with her good leg. Wrapping her fingers around the handle of the gun, she rolled over and pointed it at him. She pulled the trigger, but he kicked her, making the bullet go wide.

She tried again and all it did was click. The chamber was empty. "Shit."

Craig pounced, yanking the gun away from her. Standing up, he grabbed her by the hair and pulled her towards the tunnel.

"Someone, help me!" she yelled, grabbing at a root sticking out of the ground.

"No one's going to hear you. It's just going to be you and me forever, darling," he said, giving her head a hard tug.

As they reached the tunnel, the sound of another gun preparing to fire had Craig spinning in the opposite direction, dropping his grip on her hair.

"Freeze!" the newcomer yelled.

Her vision faded as Craig dove into the tunnel, out of sight. She heard some commotion around her, and then that was it. Nothing. Only black empty space as her eyes closed.

"Clyde, stay with her. Call for an emergency e-vac," Johnathan ordered.

"Will do."

"Peter, you're with me," Johnathan said.

John cautiously made his way down the stairs first and into the tunnel, stopping in mid stride when he saw Derek lying on the ground in a pool of blood. "Damn."

When he found out that Derek was actually Craig's foster brother, and Derek's real name was Jesse Fields, all the pieces of the puzzle fell together. He finally knew how she disappeared without a trace. They were working together. If it wasn't for his dead ex-partner, he never would have found them.

John's skills didn't rival Phillips. That was abundantly clear. If his skills had been anywhere close to his ex-partners, Jenna would have been home already. It was definitely time to consider retirement. Stepping over Derek's body, he moved through the room, keeping his eyes trained for movement.

He and Peter reached the door on the other side and stood on either side of it. Nodding his head, they stepped into the hallway, facing opposite directions, ready to fire. Footsteps echoed down the long corridor.

Covering each other's back, they moved toward the noise. As they closed in on Craig, the man turned and fired at them. Returning fire, Johnathan and Peter ducked into a side room.

John lifted his radio to his lips. "Fox-2 to all units. He is underground and on the run. Keep your eyes open," Clipping the radio back onto his belt, he volleyed a few more gunshots down the hallway and Craig did the same. John barely pulled his head back in the door when a bullet zipped past the room.

Soon, Craig stopped firing and they could hear his footsteps as he started running again. They stepped out of the room and took off after him. When they reached a fork in the path, they paused.

"Damn." Johnathan hated splitting up, but had no choice. This had to end now. "Peter, take the right. I'll go left."

"You sure?"

"No. But what other choice do we have?"

"Let's do this."

Nodding his head, they went in separate directions.

Fuming, Craig couldn't believe his brother had turned on him, especially after everything he'd done for him. He should have learned his lesson a long time ago that family was not to be trusted.

The idiot had led the police right to his door, and now he lost his most test-worthy subject. He hadn't planned on hurting her, not really, but once Derek gave his identity away, there was nothing else he could do. He couldn't let her go free and identify him. That wasn't the plan. Now he'd have to change his identity again.

First, he had to get the pigs off his back. But which way could he go? His main exit was blocked so he couldn't disappear into the forest. The only other exit nearby was the one that led into the cabin.

Maybe he could hide in the attic until they left. That was, if they weren't already inside.

Slowly, he climbed the ladder and opened the hatch. He poked his head through and found the room empty, but the front door was wide open. After closing the trapdoor behind him, he quietly looked out the front door..

From what he could tell, there were only two cops outside. They were circling the perimeter. Suddenly, their radios squawked and their heads turned towards the cabin.

"Oh, balls," he grumbled.

Moving towards the bathroom, he shoved the ceiling tiles aside and climbed up into the rafters. After replacing the panels, he leaned against the wall with every intention of staying there until they were gone.

Closing his eyes, his brother's image formed before him. He'd always felt bad for the kid, which was why he allowed Derek to hang out with him and his friends all the time. And when his dad shipped Derek off to another home after Craig's mother died, he'd been furious.

They wouldn't even tell him where he was or how to get in touch with him. They tore his brother away from him and then locked him up when he lost it. That was when he decided to become a master of technology. No one was going to keep him from his family.

Now he wished he would have let it go. They both would have been better off. He'd never been this close to being caught before. *Stupid. Stupid. Stupid.* Craig should never have let Derek in on the plan, but it was the only way to get Jenna to the cabin. And his brother had jumped on the chance to ride in like a white knight. What surprised him most was the fact that Derek wanted in on some of the action before pretending to rescue her. That was something Craig never expected.

He was actually a good-hearted, law-abiding kid, but years in the foster system, jumping from family to family, had a way of changing a person. The workers always thought they were helping the kids involved, but nothing really helped the feeling of being abandoned by your own family.

That was a feeling he knew all too well. He may have been nineteen when his dad left him at the hospital, but he'd never forgotten it. Even now, he had no idea what his dad was doing or where he lived, or if he was even alive. He honestly didn't care.

On second thought, maybe if his dad was still alive, he should be his next victim. Craig would certainly get a laugh out of making his dad squirm for once, instead of the other way around. There was never any love in his eyes or his voice. Kids were more like an inconvenience to him than anything else. Something his father put up with for the sake of his wife.

"Asshole," he muttered as he bunched his fists on his lap. *Keep it cool, dude.* He needed a level head if he was going to get out of this in one piece. It shouldn't be too hard to outsmart the cops. They weren't even smart enough to bring a dog.

As if he jinxed himself by saying the words, a loud, deep bark sounded from outside. He swallowed hard and groaned. God. This was all Derek's fault. They had to have followed his brother up here. No one had ever found him before.

It wasn't long before the trapdoor in the cabin banged open, and then slam closed. "He has to be here somewhere," a voice said.

"Don't worry, boss. We'll find him."

"I'm going to kill that son of a bitch."

Craig bit his tongue to keep from laughing nervously. No one had ever been able to kill him yet, but he'd never been this close to being captured, either. He didn't like the feeling one bit. He felt like a rabbit boxed in with nowhere to go.

Pulling his gun out of his shirt, he stared at it. Did he want to spend the rest of his life in jail? Was he ready to become another man's plaything? He was the player, not the other way around. No one was going to put him behind bars, not if he had anything to say about it.

Who would have thought he'd be the one on the other side of his own deadly game? That wasn't something he had expected. He was the one in control. The one pulling the cards from the deck and making things happen, leading people off the deep end.

"Oh well." He held the gun up to his temple and pulled the trigger.

CHAPTER TWENTY-FOUR

The sound was too quiet for the human ear to hear, but the dog heard it from outside and pulled his handler into the building. With his nose to the ground, the dog wandered through the cabin. When he entered the bathroom, he put his front paws up on the sink and sniffed the air. Giving a small whine, he promptly sat down.

"Yo, boss, he's found something," his k9 handler, Mark, said.

John raised his gun and motioned for them to leave the small room so he could look around. The cabinet under the sink wasn't big enough for anyone to hide, and the shower curtain was pulled back, showing no one was there.

Kneeling at the door of the bathroom, he ran his fingers along the wooden floor, checking for another trapdoor. Glancing at the walls, he couldn't find any sections that stood out to him. That's when he heard a slight shuffle above his head.

When he looked up, he saw a panel that was slightly out of place. It left a slight empty gap in the ceiling. *Sneaky son of a gun.* Quietly getting the attention of his men, he pointed toward the ceiling.

This was it. The time he'd been waiting for all year. His fingers itched to pull the trigger and unleash a wave of bullets into the ceiling, but he had a feeling they'd put him under review if he did. It would be quite the way to go out though, putting another creep six-feet-under so they couldn't hurt anyone else ever again. He had never wanted to kill someone so much in his life.

Taking a deep breath, he stepped out of the room and shook his head, motioning for his men to take over. He had to go outside and gather himself. The bastard took out his ex-partner, the one who'd saved his life more times than he could remember, and he had hurt an innocent girl who would likely never be the same again.

And he couldn't forget that the man took out Derek, too. How had he missed the boy's involvement? That was what rattled him the most. John had Derek in his office. He had questioned him, watched him for the usual signs of a liar. He had missed it all.

Damn it. He had the kid right in his grasp. If only he would have given him a polygraph test or did something more, maybe he'd have found her sooner and stopped all this from happening. He should have been on the ball, but maybe he was losing it in his old age.

A few minutes later, he heard a ruckus coming from inside and before long, they were dragging the perpetrator outside, hog-tied between four of his men. His feet were zip-tied together and his hands cuffed behind his back. The man was yelling at the top of his lungs.

John found himself moving toward the guy at break-neck speed, punching him square in the face, again and again. Peter and Mark took him by the arms and pulled him back.

"It's okay, boss. We got him. He can't hurt anyone else."

"You lousy son of a bitch. Where are the rest of the people you kidnapped?"

Craig, with his mouth bleeding, spat at him. A mixture of blood and spit landed on John's work shoes, and John went to tackle Craig, but his men pulled him back.

"Sir, why don't you head back to Clyde and see how things are going with the med-evac?" Peter suggested. "We'll finish up here. And don't worry, we'll do a thorough search of the area."

He was about to chew him out for telling him what to do, but he knew he'd trained them well, and that they could take care of the rest of the details. If he didn't step away now, he was liable to do exactly what he promised and send him packing to hell.

Returning to where he'd left Clyde, a voice popped up on the radio, "Fox 2-charlie to Fox-2."

"Go for Fox-2," John responded.

"We have a live one in the tunnels."

"Location?"

"The computer room."

"10-4, on my way. Clyde, what's the ETA on the med-evac?" he asked as he looked down at his partner, still cradling an unconscious Jenna.

"Should be here in a few minutes."

John put in another call for a second med-evac and then climbed into the tunnel once again.

"Report," he asked Jack, the youngest member of his team, who happened to be kneeling next to the boy, holding his hand on Derek's bleeding stomach wound.

"He's alive, but barely."

John couldn't help but wonder what went down before they arrived, but he was happy it was over. They had rescued Jenna. She was hurt, but she was alive. The man was going to go away for a very long time. The streets would once again be a little safer for everyone. And he could go into retirement a mostly happy man.

It was dark, damp and Jenna couldn't see a thing, her hands chained above her head. Her wrists were raw from all the times she had struggled to get free. He'd be back. The door could fling open at any minute, and she'd be at his mercy.

Even as she sat there, she could still feel his sticky fingers moving over her skin, branding it as his, so no one else would ever want to touch it again. It would be his forever and his face would always be there, lurking in the dark corners of her mind.

Her eyes filled and soon overflowed like fountains down her

cheeks. "Mommy," she whispered, her chin trembling. Why couldn't she have been an obedient daughter and listened to her mom? If she had, she wouldn't be in this bloody mess.

Her mom warned her not to take the job. It was almost like she had a premonition something bad was going to happen. Her mom had totally freaked out, and if it wasn't for her dad, she wouldn't have accepted the position. Jenna and her dad thought her mom was being foolish. They had brought her mom to tears by disregarding her feelings.

As she sat there reminiscing over her decision in the dark, she felt the ground slightly vibrate and a bright light filled the room. Shielding her eyes, she screamed as a shadow moved towards her.

When his hands touched her shoulders, she squeezed her eyes closed and screamed, "Leave me alone!"

Suddenly, her own hands were free, and she pushed him away, struggling to sit up. Her heart pounding so loudly she could hear the blood rushing through her body, her ears ringing.

"It's okay, Jenna. You're okay?" a faint familiar voice said from beside her.

"No. No. Go away. Go away," she cried, as someone tried to push her down.

"Open your eyes, Jenna. You're safe," the voice said again.

With her body shaking violently and her breathing erratic, she opened one eye and then the other. The room was blurry, but next to her she could make out her mother. "Mom?" she whimpered, then threw her arms around her, crying.

Her mother joined her on the bed and held her close, whispering gentle comforting words into her ear. Jenna cried so hard she hiccuped. Her mom ran her hand soothingly up and down her back, like she used to do when Jenna woke up from a nightmare.

"Oh, Mom, it was awful," she said, burying her face against her mother's chest.

Her father came over and sat down on the other side of the bed and reached out to hold her too, but when he touched her arm, Jenna shoved him away.

"Get away!" she yelled. "Don't touch me."

A frown washed over his features, and his shoulders slumped as he shoved his hands in his pockets, but he did as she asked. Despair flooded through her as she realized she'd just hurt the only man who had ever really loved her. But she couldn't handle the touch of his rough, calloused hand. A nurse came into the room after hearing the commotion.

"Where is the *bastard* that did this to my daughter?" Daniel demanded, his voice booming. Jenna let out a small cry and her mother cradled her in her arms.

"Sir, we're going to have to ask you to calm down for your daughter's sake," the nurse said.

"Just tell me where he is."

"One is in police custody."

"And the other?"

"We can't tell you. It's confidential," the nurse said, her voice squeaking nervously.

"I'm going down to the police station, Iris. I'll come back and pick you up soon." Her father stormed out of the room, leaving all of them staring after him.

It wasn't long before Jenna tried to move again and cringed as shooting pain took her breath away. The nurse noticed her grimace and said, "I'll go get you some pain meds."

"How bad is it?" Jenna asked, lifting the covers and seeing her leg in a cast.

Her mom squeezed her hand. "The doctors said you should make a full recovery, but you do need to stay off your leg for a few weeks. They have also set you up with a therapist who said they would be by later today."

"Please, Mom, can't I just go home?" she begged.

"I'd love to take you home, but they want to keep you for a few days," her mom said.

Jenna watched as her mom pulled a small box covered in pink wrapping paper. "What's that?"

Her mom let out a heavy sigh, her shoulders sagging. "There is something I should have told you a long time ago, but it hurt too much to talk about it. And when you disappeared, I realized this secret would have died with us and it wouldn't have been fair to you."

"What are you talking about?"

"I realize this isn't the happiest of Christmas presents, but you deserve to have it."

She took the small box from her mom and carefully unwrapped the paper, trying hard not to rip it. She uncovered a navy blue jewelry box. Upon opening it, she saw a golden heart-shaped locket. Taking it out of the box, she opened it and her eyes fell upon two baby pictures. She tilted her head and looked at her mother questioningly.

Tears filled her mom's eyes as she ran her fingers over the baby picture on the right. "You always asked me why I was so protective of you. She was the reason."

"Who are they?"

"It is you and Rebecca, your twin sister."

Jenna stared at the photos, dumbfounded. "I have a sister?"

Her mother opened her mouth to speak, but started crying instead. Jenna would have wrapped her arms around her, but she was frozen in place, shocked at the news.

"Where is she?" she asked, her stomach fluttering with angry butterflies.

"You guys were born premature. She didn't make it," her mother said softly, tears running down her face. "I couldn't save her. There was nothing I could do."

Suddenly, her mother's behavior all made sense, and her heart softened. All this time, she had thought her mother was a control freak, not wanting her to have any fun. "Why didn't you tell me about her?"

"It hurt too much to even think about. I know I should have, but I couldn't bring myself to even mention her name. And when you disappeared, it all came flooding back. Every hurt, every memory that I had locked away."

Jenna couldn't decide whether to be angry with her for keeping such a big secret or feeling sorry for what she'd been through. In the end, she'd placed her hands on top of her mother's and pressed her forehead against hers.

"I'm sorry, mom." And she was, for all that had happened and for all that she'd believed wrongly about her mother's behavior.

"And I'm sorry, dear, for not being the mother I should have been and for what you've been through."

Wrapping their arms around each other, they cried together, with their hearts uniting in a way that had previously been lost. The road ahead wouldn't be easy, that Iris knew, but they would endure it together. And, hopefully, grow closer to each other as only a mother and her adult daughter could.

"I know it's a few hours early, but Merry Christmas, Mom."

"Merry Christmas, Jenna."

Kissing her daughter on the cheek, she raised her eyes to the heavens and thanked God for bringing her baby home. There was no better Christmas present than that. Life was finally looking up.

EPILOGUE

T*hree Months later...*

The courtroom was silent as the audience waited for the judge to announce the sentence. When John's team searched the cabin and the underground tunnels, they found four bodies in a freezer, and a bunch of evidence of his experiments in the computer lab. Craig, or rather Mathew, was being charged for at least ten of the disappearances.

He wished it wasn't just Mathew in the courtroom waiting to be sentenced, though. He'd wanted to see Derek, or more accurately, Jesse, get the book thrown at him, too. But, the kid didn't survive and died en route to the hospital.

He looked over at Jenna, who was huddled next to her mom, head resting on her shoulder. Questioning her had been the hardest thing he'd ever done. The two men, Mathew and Jesse, were true psychos, and it made him nauseous just thinking about what Jenna had been through.

"In the case of Mathew Graham versus the crown. We find the

defendant guilty of 1st degree murder, abduction, sexual assault, attempted murder and fraud, and is hereby sentenced to life in prison, without the opportunity of parole. Take him away," the judge said, throwing his gavel down.

Jenna buried her face in her mom's chest, crying. No more testifying. No more having to tell her story to crowds of people she didn't know. She couldn't even remember how many times she'd had to tell every detail of her experience.

Every time she opened her mouth to talk about it, she'd have nightmares. She'd freeze, unable to continue. There were numerous times that she'd excused herself to run to the bathroom and puke.

The crowds all cheered and even threw paper balls at Craig, but she just sat there, cuddling with her mom. Her dad kept his hands to himself and for that, she was grateful. She still couldn't handle him touching her. The therapist tried to encourage her to give him a hug, or at least hold his hand, but even the thought made her stomach churn.

The hurt in his eyes killed her, and she desperately wanted to reach out to him, but her hands wouldn't listen. Her body curled away from him automatically. "I'm sorry, Dad," she whispered.

With a tight smile, he nodded his head before turning to stare at the man they were leading away.

Crying even harder as guilt assailed her, her mom rubbed her back. "Shhh, he can't hurt you anymore, darling."

Her mom didn't understand that it wasn't over for Jenna. That the pain was still there, as strong as ever. Every night, she faced it all over again when her dream world became a nightmare. She hated to go to bed, didn't want to sleep, didn't want to dream. Now her latest nightmare came true, and she had yet to tell her parents.

She watched as Craig disappeared through the door, being led away in handcuffs. Jenna had hoped seeing him convicted would make her feel better, but it didn't. There was no significant change in the darkness she felt. And she knew why. Because for her, it wasn't over. It would never be over.

"Excuse me." She shoved her way down the aisle and bolted out of the courtroom, taking refuge in the washroom nearby. Locking herself in the stall, she puked for the fifth time that day.

Once her body settled, she stepped outside and stared at herself in the mirror, her strawberry blond hair in mass disarray, her eyes bloodshot. She didn't know what to do. Didn't know how to make the nightmare end. She'd rather die than face the decision she had on her hands.

Iris stepped into the washroom behind her, resting her hands on Jenna's shoulder.

"Mom, I have something to tell you," she said, turning in her mom's arms. "I'm pregnant."

To be continued in Beneath His Hands...

INTERNATIONAL AND AWARD-WINNING AUTHOR

PATRICIA ELLIOTT

...Patricia offers a nuanced exploration of human relationships filled with engaging and multi-faceted characters that will keep readers captivated until the last page.

Literary Titan

To read more from this author, please visit:

https://patriciaelliottromance.com/books

NEWSLETTER

Join Patricia Elliott's *where love meets suspense* newsletter. She'll be sharing updates about her current books, upcoming releases, exclusive content, and more. You'll also have the opportunity to contact her and ask whatever questions your heart desires. Currently, you'll also receive a short story called, **"Into the Fire,"** for free.

Blurb:

Ash Daniels is single and plans to stay that way. Theresa Martin, the only woman he ever loved, left him high and dry, disappearing from his life years ago without a trace. Now, his only focus is saving his town from a raging bushfire that has sorted the land all around them. When he's dispatched to his ex-girlfriend's place, his painful past comes rushing forward. His only hope is that he can stay focused long enough to save her place and not die in the process.

Theresa Martin never expects to face a life or death situation; but, when the bushfire reaches her backyard, she realizes that the secret she's been keeping isn't hers to keep anymore. She has to tell Ash why she ran away before death rips that chance away.

But what he'll do with the news is anyone's guess…